THE MORNING AFTER

SALLY CLEMENTS

The Morning After

By Sally Clements

Large Print Edition ISBN: 9798861315425

LARGE PRINT

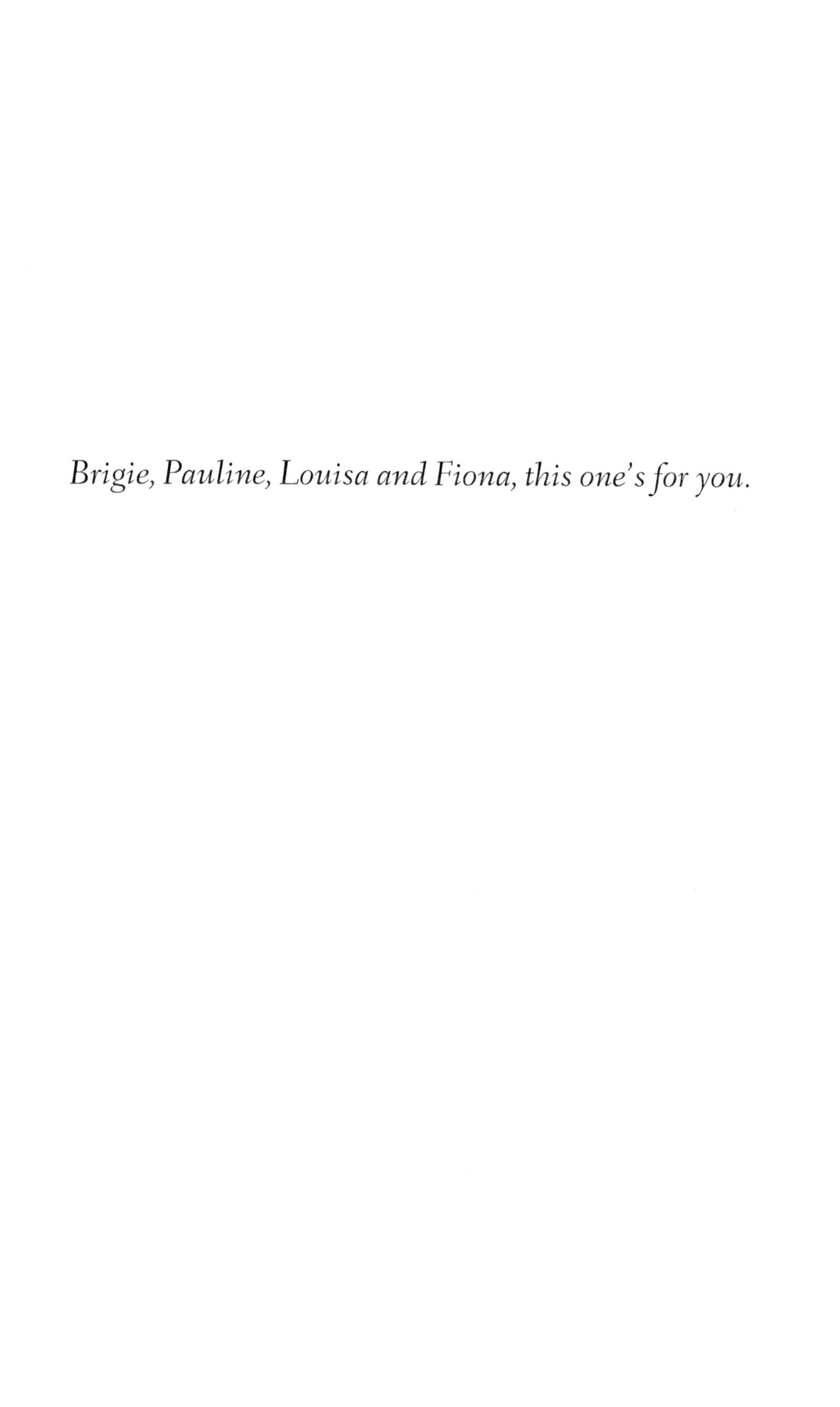

Brigie, Pauline, Louisa and Fiona, this one's for you.

ONE

He was tall. Blond. Good looking. With his arm around a curvy brunette, and his tongue in her mouth. A place it had no business being.

Heat flashed through Ethan Quinn as he slammed his pint on the table. "Excuse me for a moment." He stood from the upholstered seat, half hidden from view in a shady corner, and pushed his way through the crowd on the dance floor. He'd never been in this particular club before, but his brother Sean had wanted to come and hear the smoky-voiced jazz singer visiting from Canada, and it had seemed as good a place as any to catch up.

As he approached, a wave of anger flooded Ethan at the sight of Michael's hand edging toward the pretty brunette's breast. Holding her in a full-body clinch, he was dirty dancing as if his life depended on it.

Ethan tapped his shoulder.

Michael's head jerked up. His eyes widened, then a smile lifted the corners of his mouth as recognition struck. "Hi..."

It was the smile that did it. The smile that presumed collusion. That Ethan wouldn't be furious to find his best friend's almost fiancé snuggling up to another woman mere days after he'd proposed. The smile that gave lie to the promise he'd made to choose only her for the rest of his miserable life.

Ethan's fist connected with Michael's jaw.

The brunette screamed.

The singer's voice faltered and died mid note, and the music degenerated into a haphazard discordant collection of sound, before stuttering to a halt.

Ethan nursed his bruised knuckles, feeling the dull pain of impact all the way to his elbow. Two bouncers were on Ethan instantly, grabbing his arms with painful grips.

"Out," a black suited gorilla muttered.

"Oh, believe me, I'm going." Ethan glared at the man sprawled on the ground before him. "Break it off—or I tell her." He laced just enough menace in his tone to ensure Michael knew he wasn't kidding. Cara didn't need a husband who was a love-rat. No decent woman needed that. Ethan turned to the bouncer. "I've done what I needed to do."

Sean met him outside. "I thought the plan was to go incognito." Sean's forehead creased in a frown. "Punching out some random guy is hardly low key."

Ethan rubbed his stinging knuckles, then stretched his fingers in a tentative flex. "He's no random guy. That's Cara's man."

Sean's eyes widened. "Ah, no." A blast of music blared through the door as it opened and a crowd of revelers exited. "Let's get out of here."

They parted at Ethan's rented BMW.

"I'll catch up with you tomorrow." Regret niggled that their catch-up time had been cut short, but Sean was on duty in the morning—the last thing he needed was a late night bender with his older brother.

"Just try not to get into any more trouble." Sean grinned. "I don't want to have to arrest you. You're not supposed to even be here until tomorrow afternoon. You can't afford the publicity..."

"I know." Ethan rubbed his hand through his overlong hair, hating the feel of it flopping over his face. But he couldn't cut it—there was still another week and a half of filming before he could return to his usual crop.

Sometimes being famous sucked.

And tomorrow he'd have to talk to Cara. Tell her, before someone else did. A fat raindrop splattered on the car roof. Doubtless the first of many. Ethan zipped his leather jacket, tugged open the car door, and ducked inside, feeling a grimace on his face.

By the time he drove onto the motorway, the windscreen wipers were struggling to keep up with the driving rain. *Typical Irish weather.* He flicked on the radio, and turned up the heat, heart heavy as he headed for the anonymity of his rented hotel room.

SWEAT TRICKLED down Cara Byrne's spine. She wriggled inside the heavy costume, wishing she could somehow free a hand to scratch, then gave up in disgust as the heavy head wobbled. She couldn't even see in this thing. Why, oh why, had she consented to dress up for the fundraiser?

As a member of the organizing committee, there were plenty of jobs she could have chosen. She could have manned the coconut shy. Could have snagged the job of handing out goldfish to kids who managed to win one throwing hoops, if Caitlin Murphy hadn't leapt in there first.

Instead, she'd been late to the huge fairground set-up on the one patch of green in the middle of Donabridge, and as a result been stuck with the last job going. The one nobody wanted. That of dressing up as Winnie the Pooh.

She shuffled toward the huge wall where she was supposed to do her thing. If she hadn't been so distracted by Ethan's message, she would be handing out goldfish instead of sweltering in the midsummer heat in a small town in County Kildare.

She stopped short as an ice cream-clutching kid almost knocked her over.

She'd been in the shower when Ethan called. Then been frantically multitasking. Bread in the toaster—she could eat it on the way. Hairdryer on, blasting heat, which would leave her hair in a thick blonde cloud. Yet through it all she'd heard the beep signaling a missed message.

His recorded voice had sounded so strange. "Cara? Pick up. It's Ethan. Pick up." Silence had stretched for long moments. "Oh, dammit." His voice lowered. "Are you okay? I'll see you at the fair. I'll explain everything when I see you."

Cara'd called him back straight away. But his cell phone had flicked to voicemail, indicating he'd turned it off. Which was so not like him. No matter what his mood, he always had his cell on. His assistant needed instant access.

A hand grabbed the arm of her bulky costume. "Here you are."

The hand pulled her to an elaborate wall with a hole carefully carved in its centre.

"Okay, now you know what you're supposed to be doing, right?" Caitlin's sweet voice wafted up from a hidden point to her left. "You're Winnie the Pooh. And you've gone through the hole into Rabbit's house to eat his honey, eaten too much, and got stuck. I've got the honey pots stacked up here, all we need is you stuck in the wall."

"Yes, I understand." Cara wished the day was over, and it hadn't even begun. There were three long hours before she could climb out of this ridiculous costume.

"Can't hear you!" Caitlin's voice rang out. She even had the cheek to giggle.

Cara clenched her teeth.

"Bend over; I'll help you into position."

It was like trying to pee in a bucket blindfolded. Not impossible, but darned difficult.

"Okay, now put your arms out," Caitlin said. "And step forward."

Cara did so with her arms extended and her back bent, thinking what an idiot she must look. Thank goodness Michael couldn't see her. He was working—spending long hours in the office.

He was very conscientious. That's probably why all her family thought he was perfect for her. Solid, stable, and a good bet. Not her type at all, really, she'd always had a thing for hell-raisers. Dad liked him. Mum liked him. Even Ryan and Finn liked him, and they'd never liked any of the men she went out with before.

But despite her family's seal of approval, she just couldn't persuade herself to accept his proposal of marriage. He was gorgeous and sexy, but somehow...

Her thighs rubbed against the costume's rough interior.

They'd messed around, but hadn't slept together yet. There'd been plenty of opportunity, but something was lacking. A spark.

She'd hidden that fact from Ethan when she rang to tell him of Michael's proposal. He would have asked the question she really didn't want to answer—*Why?*

To Ethan, being involved with someone definitely meant taking them to bed. It wasn't as though she hadn't made love before. She'd thrown herself headlong into a passionate affair with Dev

Coonan when she was barely out of her teens, and look how *that* ended.

The very first time she trusted a man enough to stretch her wings, she'd crashed and burned when a spiked drink had led to a drunk and disorderly arrest. The weasely Dev had made his escape quickly, leaving her stumbling on the road outside the pub. Since then she'd wised up. There would be no more bad boys for her. And now that she'd finally finished her training and got a sensible job teaching English in The Donabridge Secondary School for boys, she couldn't risk any hint of scandal.

She really should consider Michael's proposal. After all, he was hardly likely to have proposed if he didn't love her, was he?

An insecure little voice inside whispered words of doubt. *Michael's ambitious,* the poisonous voice sneered. *And you're the boss's daughter.*

Her musings were interrupted by a sharp push from behind. Cara cursed in an unladylike way, liberated in the knowledge that Caitlin couldn't hear.

"That's perfect! You're half in." Caitlin laughed. "Wow, you look just perfect. Absolutely huge ass though!"

"Thanks," Cara muttered. At least there was no need for Caitlin to stick around and torment her any further. She could go back to her goldfish, leaving Cara crouched over, waving her arms around and tilting her head to make Pooh look 'real' for half an hour. Then she'd have a break.

Caitlin hadn't gone. "I'm so excited. Imagine, the premiere and the dinner are tonight!"

Cara indulged in an over-the-top eye roll.

"I remember Ethan from school, although he was so much older than me," she continued. "He was in your class wasn't he? And he's such a hunk. I wonder if he'll remember me."

Women world over wished Ethan would remember them. They always had. Long before he'd taken to the screen as Crash Carrigan in a number of action hero roles. And seduced every one of his leading ladies.

Cara felt a grin on her lips.

She must be the only woman in the world who was immune to his spell. Ever since the first day in secondary school when they sat next to each other. Ethan hadn't been like the other kids. Instead of joking around and hanging out after class, he kept to himself. He was small for his age. And his Dublin accent set him apart in a classroom of boys, who had known each other all their lives.

It had taken months for her to discover that he had a younger brother, still in primary school. Cara'd seen his mother—a pale, thin woman—with them at the shops sometimes. But she'd seen no sign of his father, no one had. But she knew.

She'd worked it out the day she went in to the hospital where her mother was a doctor, and saw Ethan waiting for his drunken father to be discharged from the emergency room.

Cara shifted in the heavy costume. Puffed a targeted breath to flick the hair out of her eyes. It smelled in here too, of moldy fake fur and sweat. A dull ache bloomed in her back. Surely it must be time for a break? She tugged backwards.

The costume didn't move.

Panic welled up as she tugged again. She peered out through the viewing slot in the mask's wide mouth, unable to see more than a sliver in front of her. A sliver filled with people passing by, and a small boy standing between smiling parents. He pointed at her head, and wiggled with excitement. "Look, it's Pooh!"

Cara cartwheeled her arms frantically.

"He's waving!" The high voice pealed out, and the toddler waved back.

His parents smiled indulgently. Handed him a bucket of popcorn and turned away.

Caitlin hadn't been able to hear her earlier, but maybe if she shouted..."Help!"

They kept walking.

Cara breathed in a ragged breath. *Great.* No

one could hear her. Knowing the heat inside the costume would be unbearable, she'd stripped to her bra and panties in the changing room. Her cell phone was in her jeans pocket. She couldn't even call anyone. *Could this day get any worse?*

TWO

She still wasn't answering her blasted cell.

Ethan called Sean. Like most of the local gardai he was on duty in the park. He'd know where she was. He didn't bother with small talk. "Do you know where Cara is?"

"Hang on."

Ethan heard Sean on his radio, but couldn't make out the words.

He slipped his arms into his hoodie and zipped it up, feeling the stretch of his angled neck, which kept the phone crushed between jaw and shoulder.

"She's Winnie the Pooh."

Ethan stilled. *Winnie the Pooh?* "What?"

"She's dressed as a bear as part of a display. Winnie the Pooh. You know, the one with Eeyore and Christopher Robin." Sean laughed. "She wasn't very happy about it."

Silence for a moment.

"I can see her from the window—she's stuck through a wall next to a pile of honey pots. She's waving her arms around."

Ethan grinned. She'd hate that. No wonder she wasn't answering his calls, no doubt she couldn't reach her cell phone. She was such a trooper. Even with her heart breaking, she'd still got out there, when any normal person would have welshed on the deal and stayed at home to lick their wounds.

There was nothing for it. He'd have to go find her.

Ethan flicked the hood of his sweatshirt up and slipped on his wraparound shades.

Ten minutes later, he was strolling head down through the crowds that thronged the park. Couples with kids were everywhere. The air smelt of hot-dogs and candyfloss, and the sun shone down, all traces of the previous night's rain long soaked away into the ground. To his relief no one cast him a second glance. They weren't expecting him until the premiere and fundraising dinner later, and the last place people would expect to see a Hollywood movie star was in the park in the centre of town.

A grin stretched his mouth the moment he saw her. The huge yellow head and arms of the cartoon bear stuck through the wall, and despite the fact that her arms were flapping around like sails in a storm, most people didn't even stop to appreciate her efforts.

Ethan stood in front of the ridiculous bear, slipped off his shades, and stared into the wide-spaced plastic eyes. She couldn't possibly see through those. He peered lower, eventually spotting a thin slit in the centre of the mouth. He moved close, and squatted. "Are you in there?"

Familiar bright blue eyes ringed with dark lashes blinked. "Urrr."

"What?" Ethan leaned close and pressed his ear against the furry costume.

"Urrr!"

It sounded as though she was cross. Or panicked.

"Are you all right in there?" He stared at her eyes. They widened. Then fluttered. Three fast blinks, three slow ones, then three fast ones again.

SOS? They'd drummed it on the desk in class often enough, a warning to sit back down at their desks and pretend to be working when a teacher was on the way back to the classroom.

A frown line could just be seen between Cara's eyebrows.

A cold fist clenched at Ethan's insides. There

was something wrong. He knew it. "Wave your arms if you're in trouble."

A huge hand crashed against his head as the giant fluffy figure waved wildly.

"Okay, Cara. Don't panic." Ethan pushed back the hood of his sweatshirt and rubbed his head. "I'll get you out of there."

Easier said than done.

Ethan tugged at the back of the unwieldy costume for the umpteenth time, then gave up in defeat. The arms and head were thoroughly wedged in the hole. There was no way she was getting loose unless he took down the wall around her. And someone had gone to a great deal of trouble to make it out of brick. The danger was, in taking it down she'd be injured by falling rubble.

His efforts were gaining attention too. A small crowd was forming, watching him pull and push. He scooted around to the head again, and peered through the crack. "Well you're stuck alright."

Her baby blues stared back.

He stepped away, and carefully examined the front of the costume, searching for the seam that separated the head from the body.

"I'm taking the head off."

Grasping the ears, Ethan tugged firmly, falling backwards onto the ground with the head clasped to his chest.

The watching crowd cheered.

There was no point ignoring them any longer. Ethan tossed the head to the side, bowed to the crowd, and grinned.

"God, you took your time," Cara moaned.

She'd cut her hair since his last visit home a year ago. It barely reached her shoulders now; bangs were plastered to her damp forehead. Her mascara had run, giving her panda eyes.

"I'm glad to see you though." She gave smiling a try, rather unconvincingly.

Her lip wobbled. Was that a hint of moisture in her eyes?

Ethan strode forward. "I'm going to pull you out. Can you get your hands free?"

The costume was so huge, her head and shoulders were plainly visible within the gaping hole. He could reach in, get his hands under her armpits...Ethan blinked. Her *naked* armpits. He put his head close to hers, and peered down into the costume's shadowy depths. "What are you wearing?"

Cara clenched her eyes tight. "Nothing."

A vivid vision of Cara naked flashed in Ethan's mind, heating his blood and causing his whole body to tense instantly. He gritted his teeth, and forced himself to think of something else. *Anything* except his best friend naked. "Tell me you're kidding," he hissed in a deep voice.

"I'm kidding." The corner of her mouth turned up in an unconvincing smile. "But only just. I'm in my underwear."

A bead of sweat trickled down her forehead.

Ethan glanced around. Now that Winnie The Pooh's head was off, the little crowd had lost interest, and had wandered over to watch the pop group that was tuning up on the other side of the park. He needed to get her out of here. And there was only one way to do it. "I hope you're wearing your pretty set, rather than your granny knickers."

Cara's eyes widened.

"Stick your arms out." Ethan reached in through the open head of the costume and rested his hands on her bare shoulders. A shot of electricity flashed through his hands up his arms and jump-started his heart into a frantic drum-roll. His fingers curled convulsively around Cara's softly curved shoulders. What on earth was going on? He'd never had that reaction touching Cara before; she was the one woman in the world he wasn't attracted to in that way...

But now, staring into the azure pools of her eyes, he felt like he was drowning.

Her tongue swept across her bottom lip.

And desire blazed through Ethan like a forest

fire. The urge to taste her lips welled up out of nowhere. Attraction simmered in the air between their bodies. She was feeling it too; her expanding irises and sudden stillness were testament to that.

Cara glanced away. "So, how's this going to work?"

Her words threw him into confusion. It couldn't work, her relationship had just gone belly-up, and he...he never had long-term relationships. He cleared his throat.

Cara frowned. "Ethan, get me out of this damn costume." Her voice held an edge of panic.

Reality seeped through the fog in his brain. Of course, she wasn't talking about their shifting relationship, she was talking about something much more urgent. The need to get her free.

She wriggled, then both her arms slipped through the opening. Ethan bent and slid his hands down to her ribcage, grasping her firmly. Her hands linked behind his neck.

"Ready?" He tried not to react to the feel of her breath against his cheek. Clenched his teeth tight to force the attraction onto the back burner.

"Ready," she whispered.

With one huge effort, Ethan pulled her from the costume.

Her face was against his neck. Her chest

melded to his as she shimmied out of the confining suit into his arms.

Her legs were half in, half out, and he slipped an arm around her bottom and jerked. Arms full of half-naked warm woman, Ethan closed his eyes for a moment and breathed in her musky scent.

TALK *about out of the frying pan into the fire.* Every inch of Cara's body was pressed hard against Ethan's. His long hair brushed against the backs of her fingers. Her lips were at his strong column of neck, and her breasts were squashed against his hard expanse of chest.

One hand held onto her bottom, and a flush of heat bloomed in her stomach at the contact.

This. This was what was missing in her relationship with Michael. How could she even consider marrying someone who didn't arouse such exciting feelings in her? She didn't want Ethan to let her go. She wanted to rip off his T-shirt and feel his naked flesh against hers. Wanted to kiss him, long and deep, and wrap her legs around his waist.

Rapid fire clicking.

Ethan cursed loudly. He slid her down his body to the ground. Her legs wobbled as her Converse All stars settled on the damp grass.

Ethan ripped off his hoodie. "Put it on." He held it open as she slipped her arms into the oversized garment. And stood quiet as a child as his long tanned fingers slipped the tab home, and zipped up to her neck.

He glanced at her bare legs. "Come on, let's get out of here."

"My clothes..."

Ethan's dark chocolate gaze searched hers. "Where?"

Cara pointed. "In the trailer."

Ethan's arm circled her waist. He strode across the field so fast she had to jog to keep up. "We need to get out of here. Someone was taking photographs." He glanced behind them, his strong jaw clenched tight.

Everywhere he went people took photographs.

Cara bit her bottom lip. How on earth would she explain the picture to Michael? And her parents—who were so ready to see the worst in every situation after that wild incident in her past?

"Grab your stuff," Ethan demanded as they reached the trailer. "Don't hang around to change. You can pick your car up later, I'll bring mine around."

Ten minutes later they were in his car, speeding through the country roads to the cottage she rented on the outskirts of town. Dappled sunlight streaks flashed through the windscreen, cast by the avenue of tall beeches straddling the road. Cara's jeans were inside out. She tried to untangle them, then gave up, and leaned back against the seat's warm leather interior.

"They're going to wonder where I've gone." No doubt the sight of a headless Winnie the Pooh would cause nightmares tonight for some of the toddlers who came across it. She couldn't make herself care though. Being stuck inside the dark costume had been terrible. And when she'd seen Ethan's familiar face she'd thought she'd faint with relief.

Something beeped in the pile of clothes on her lap. "I must have a message," she said.

"You missed at least five from me," Ethan said. "I've been trying to contact you all morning."

Curiosity niggled. "I'm coming to the premiere and the dinner, why would you need to get hold of me so urgently?"

Ethan's hands tightened on the steering wheel. He gazed through the windshield, and jerked his head as her cottage came into view. "This is you, right?"

The niggle turned into an ache. "Yes." She'd only seen Ethan so serious once or twice in the years since they'd been friends. When there was trouble.

The powerful car surged up the driveway, then came to a stop at her cherry-red front door. "We'll talk inside."

In the tiny kitchen, Cara dumped her clothes onto the heavy pine table. "Put the kettle on, then. I'll get dressed." She turned her back. But still felt his gaze on her.

He didn't move.

She swiveled to face him. "Ethan?"

His dark brown eyes, fringed with lashes so long they were positively indecent on a man stared into hers. His long hair flopped across his forehead, and he pushed it back with a tanned hand. His mouth...

Cara couldn't seem to stop looking at his mouth.

When he spoke it was in a tortured rasp. "Have you spoken to Michael today?"

Cara closed her eyes. Guilt sliced through her like a knife. *What was the matter with her?* Michael Maguire, the man who wanted to marry her, hadn't even flickered through her mind since Ethan had appeared. She was having naughty fantasies about having her very own steamy Crash Carrigan love scene in her kitchen, when she should be having those fantasies about Michael. And she'd never, ever fancied Ethan before.

Heat flushed her cheeks. "I haven't spoken to Michael since yesterday afternoon," she muttered. "He's been working." She fumbled with the clothes on the table, pulling out her cell-phone. Six missed calls, and a couple of text messages. "He's probably been trying to get in contact with me too."

Ethan stepped close. So close her nipples peaked beneath his sweatshirt. His hand cupped her jaw as he tilted her face up to his.

"I've something to tell you."

THREE

Cara jerked away from Ethan's hand. She took a step back, a frown creasing between her eyebrows. Her pixie chin tilted up in a familiar 'go on then, I'm braced for it' challenge.

Ethan swallowed. Ridiculous as it was, that look from this pocket Venus was enough to make him wish he was somewhere else. Anywhere else but standing before Cara as she waited for him to elaborate.

That look probably got her class full of teenage boys to pay attention.

Despite the fact that her legs were bare, and she was covered from shoulder to mid-thigh in his hoodie, she looked like a strong, confident woman who would balk at nothing. But they were friends.

Closer than family. And that look couldn't fool him. It masked Cara's soft center. A gentle heart that would be crushed when she learned the truth of her lover's betrayal. Ethan's hands curled into fists. "You better sit down."

Cara rolled her eyes. "Come on, Ethan." Her voice was laced with just the right amount of light scorn. Then she stilled and grasped his arm. The color bled from her face. "Oh Christ, has there been an accident? Is Michael..."

Why was he making such a mess of this?

Ethan shook his head. "He's fine." He helped her onto the nearest chair, and sat down opposite her, pulling his chair close so their knees were touching. "But he's not the guy you think he is."

Cara's shoulders stiffened.

Ethan took a deep breath, and prepared himself for breaking her heart. "I came into town yesterday, and met up with Sean for a drink." His throat was dry—a drink right about now might be good. "Anyway, I saw Michael in the club."

"But he was working last night." Cara's voice was barely louder than a whisper.

"Maybe he told you he was working, but I saw him. With a woman."

Cara's eyes widened. She looked like a puppy that had been kicked.

Ethan's heart clenched. He knew that feeling,

only too well. He gritted his teeth, and ploughed on. She deserved to know all the gory details. "I'm telling you because you need to know." He reached for her hand and warmed it between both of his. "He was kissing the woman."

Cara gasped. The fingers captured between his hands fluttered and shook. "I..." Her head shook in rapid shakes back and forth in fervent rejection of his words.

Ethan focused all his attention on her white face. "There's no mistake." His voice was deep and quiet. "He was messing around, when he'd already asked you to be his bride."

"Did he see you?" Cara forced out through white lips.

"Yeah, about thirty seconds before I hit him." Ethan felt his mouth stretch in a tight smile.

"You hit..."

Ethan crossed his arms. "He deserved it."

A ringing cut through the silence. Ethan reached into his pocket to fish out his cell phone, pressing a button to send it to voicemail without even glancing at the display to see who was calling.

"I need to talk to him." Cara stood. She scanned the messages on her phone. "He rang me this morning and left a message. I need to listen to it."

Ethan's phone rang again.

Cara glanced at his pocket. "You better answer that, it could be important." Clutching her phone, she walked from the kitchen into the sitting room.

She was hurting. And she had more hurt on the way, when she heard confirmation from Michael's own lips.

Ethan flicked his cell phone to voicemail again, and strode into the sitting room.

Cara was curled up on the red leather sofa. The phone was clamped against her ear, and her eyes were scrunched up tight. Her free arm was wrapped around her stomach—as if holding herself together.

Ethan stopped in the doorway. Maybe he should give her some privacy. He discarded that idea the moment it formed. She didn't need privacy, she needed a friend. And luckily, she had one. "Cara."

Her eyes opened. She snapped her phone shut and placed it carefully on the sofa next to her. "He left me a message."

Ethan picked up her phone and sat down next to her. "May I?"

She nodded.

Michael's familiar voice replayed. "You've probably already heard from your friend. And yes, I won't bother to deny it. I was out with a woman.

And, as his bloody brother was there to witness it, I won't waste your time and mine in pretending it was innocent."

Ethan glanced at Cara.

She stared at the wall.

"The truth is you're a bit of a cold fish. A man needs a willing woman sometimes." Michael's voice was laced with bitterness. "I know it's over between us. Don't bother calling me back, I'm turning my phone off and going to Dublin for a few days."

Dead air filled the space where his apology should have been.

"Cara."

"I don't want to talk about it, Ethan. And I'd like you to go." Cara stood hugging herself. Avoiding his eyes.

Ethan wanted to pull her into his arms. Reassure her that everything would be all right. He wanted to tell her that Michael had always been an ass, since he'd been captain of the rugby team, always chasing girls with big breasts and come-hither eyes. But adding to her grief wouldn't help. She'd asked him to go, and he would. "The premiere is at eight," he said. "I'll be here to pick you up."

She shook her head. "I'm not going."

There was too much space between them. He

closed it, grasping her upper arms gently. "If you don't go, everyone will want to know why. You've been involved with the fundraiser for the hospital from the outset. You're on the committee. It was your idea, for God's sake. You're going. With me." He kissed her cheek. "I'll be back at seven-thirty. Be ready."

THREE HOURS and a bucket of Haagan-Dazs later, Cara wandered into her bathroom. She peered in the mirror. Swollen, bloodshot eyes peered back. With a twist of the faucet, the basin filled with cold water. She wrung out a flannel and sat on the toilet seat, flopping the wet cloth over her face.

Her shoulders relaxed as the cold water soothed. Ethan was right. If she didn't go to the premiere, everyone would want to know why. They'd call, maybe even turn up at her house to find out what was wrong. She couldn't let that happen. It would make her humiliation so much worse.

The only thing for it was to dress up in the slinky number she'd bought specially for the occasion, put a brave face on, and make some excuse for Michael's absence. The bad news could come out tomorrow. Tonight the success of the fundraiser must be her only concern.

An hour later, the doorbell rang.

Cara glanced out the bedroom window.

A long, black limousine idled by the curb, with a uniformed driver staring straight ahead. She checked herself out in the mirror. Glittery purple dress. A quick turn around made sure vpl's were absent. Matching killer heels—hopefully she wouldn't have to walk far in them. Carefully applied makeup had banished the crying jag from earlier, and her hair looked okay too—it should, she'd spent long enough taming it.

She tried out her party smile. Not great, but it'd have to do.

The doorbell rang again, obviously jabbed a couple of times in quick succession. She caught a glimpse of her first real smile in hours as she turned from the mirror. Her heart warmed. Ethan was there for her. He was always there for her. She grabbed her matching purple bag from the bed, and hurried to open the door.

"Wow." Ethan's wide grin set off a tingle of reaction in her stomach. "You look..." His gaze swept her head to toe. "Fantastic."

He looked pretty damn fantastic too, in a fitted black suit, black shirt and black silk tie. Not many men could carry off such a severe look, but with his long hair brushing his shoulders and that hint of stubble, Ethan looked every inch the Hollywood movie star.

She breathed in the scent of sandalwood and man, and a wobbly, swoony feeling swept through her. "You look pretty fantastic yourself," she whispered.

"We're well matched then." Ethan took her hand. "Ready to go?"

In the limo, Ethan carefully poured her a glass of champagne. "I thought we could do with a glass before we get there."

"Do you always have a drink before you go out to things?" Her voice sounded sharp. "I mean, you're not drinking too much, are you, Ethan?" Her hand covered his.

Ethan swallowed a mouthful. "I don't drink too much. And no, I don't usually have a drink before I go out to things."

"I didn't mean..."

His gaze burned her to her spine with its intensity. "I know what you meant," he said in a soft voice. "You were thinking of my father. But believe me, I have enough friends in the business who abuse alcohol, and I'm not inclined to become a user. I know how that can turn out." He gazed out the window.

"So the champagne's for me, then?"

At the teasing tone in her voice, Ethan turned back. "Yes. I thought you could do with some Dutch courage before facing everyone."

Cara put her glass down carefully on the built in table and reached out to trail a hand over his jaw. "Come here you."

He leaned closer.

She kissed his cheek, feeling the stubble against her lips. "You are a good friend, Ethan Quinn, and I don't think I've told you how much I appreciate you."

If his face angled, their lips would meet.

Cara pulled back. "So." She sucked in a deep breath, and forced a lightness into her voice she sure didn't feel. "You hit him. Tell me all about it."

"It was a real Crash Carrigan move. Uppercut to the jaw. He went down like a sack of potatoes."

A laugh bubbled up from somewhere deep inside, releasing the pain and angst with it as it filled the close confines of the car.

Ethan's eyes lightened. "Then I told him he better tell you—or I would."

A mental image flashed of Ethan standing over the man who'd proposed to her, eyes blazing with anger. "You said that?"

"I managed to get that in before the bouncers threw me out."

If the paparazzi had been there... Cara's heart tightened. The gossip rags would have a field day if they'd managed to snatch a photo. Ethan's every move was tracked by voracious newshounds. Every woman who appeared on his arm was automatically photographed, researched and discussed as a potential love interest.

She squeezed her hands together in her lap.

The press was covering the premiere and the dinner afterwards. She'd be the focus of attention as his date. Her mouth dried as she weighed the potential fallout.

"We're here." Ethan drained his glass.

"Don't say anything to anyone about Michael," Cara managed as the car slid to a halt outside Donabridge's one screen cinema.

"Not a word." Ethan squeezed her hand.

The chauffeur swung the door open.

The air filled with the sound of excited cheering. Earsplitting screams, and frantic clapping broke out the moment the crowd saw Ethan's face. The moment he stepped onto the red carpet and raised his arms up, the crowd behind the barriers went wild.

Cara's heart thudded as she stepped from the limo behind him. A lightning storm of flashes and the sound of a million camera clicks filled the air. *Wow*. She'd known he was popular, but somehow...

Cara glanced over. Somehow popular didn't cover half of it. Ethan was a superstar, if the over-excited followers were anything to go by.

A tall brunette dressed in a sensible pantsuit grabbed his arm, and shot Cara a 'who are you?' glance.

"Maggie, this is my date, Cara," Ethan said. "Cara, this is Maggie, my assistant."

Maggie's mouth stretched into a tight smile that didn't quite reach her eyes. "Good to meet you." She closed the door of the limo. "Let's get the two of you down that carpet."

It seemed every foot of the way Ethan slowed to respond to a shouted question. He signed autographs, shook hands with people he'd known in his childhood. And stopped to pause for photographs before the bank of assembled paparazzi.

Cara felt the prick of tears in her eyes. His mother, were she still alive, would have been so proud to see he'd finally achieved his dream. She'd taken two jobs to pay for him to attend stage school in Dublin, had been adamant that he should have every opportunity. And it had paid off. Big time.

Ethan turned and extended his hand.

The moment their hands met, brightness flickered in rapid camera flashes. He slung an arm around her waist. “You’re doing great,” he whispered in her ear.

She’d been stuck in a Winnie the Pooh costume, been betrayed by her boyfriend, and ended up on the red carpet with a Hollywood star. *What a day*.

FOUR

A moment before they reached the cinema's interior, Cara spotted both her parents, and her buoyant mood burst. She stopped dead.

Ethan turned. "Problem?"

"My parents are here. I need to talk to them."

Ethan nodded. "Okay, let's get them inside, you can talk before they let everyone else in."

With a quick word to the gardai manning the barriers, Cara's parents, Ellie and Bill, slipped through.

After greeting Ethan, Ellie Byrne turned to her only daughter. "What's going on?" she questioned in a quiet voice. "Why aren't you here with Michael?"

Cara's heart sank into her boots. The dream of having a night of denial before facing the cold truth had well and truly evaporated. Ethan was deep in conversation with her father, but his assistant hovered—obviously keen to shepherd him towards the line of waiting politicians.

"Dad." Her call caught her father's attention. "Can I talk to you for a second?" She steered them to a quiet corner. "I have to talk to you both about Michael."

Bill Byrne frowned.

Ellie Byrne's mouth turned down at the corners. She looked as though she'd swallowed a wasp. "What have you done?" her forehead pleated. "I hope you haven't thrown him over for..." she glanced Ethan's direction.

Cara opened her mouth to refute her mother's words, but before she could answer, Ellie continued. "He's a nice enough boy. And, God knows, he's had terrible problems to overcome in his life, but he's not for you, Cara."

Anger flashed. Ethan hadn't done anything to qualify as 'not for you'. The unfairness threw Cara off track. "Why not?" She squeezed her lips together. It was too late to call back her question, to steer the conversation back to her errant almost fiancé, but she really wanted to know.

"Because he's flighty. Like that other lad. He won't be one for settling down." Her mother's eyes softened. "I know you like him. You've always had a soft spot for him..."

"...but don't make the mistake of thinking he's the one for you. Not when you have a perfectly good man asking for your hand, who *is* the settling down type." Her father finished.

"Well, that's the thing," Cara said. "Michael *isn't*."

As she explained, the expression on their faces cycled through concern, disbelief, shock and slid to a halt at anger.

"So where the hell is he now?" Bill demanded. His color was high, and his hands clenched into fists.

"He said he was spending the weekend in Dublin," Cara said. Being so angry couldn't be good for his blood pressure. She squeezed his hand. "Ethan just brought me along so I wouldn't have to explain to everyone."

Ellie's arm went around Cara, holding her tight. "But we're all sitting together—they'll be an empty space," Ellie said.

"I've reorganized the table. My assistant and the lighting director will be joining you at your table, and Cara is going to sit with me."

At the voice behind her, Cara turned.

"No one will ask her any awkward questions. Not tonight anyway." Ethan slipped an arm through hers.

"But people will get the wrong idea." To Cara's dismay, her father's jaw clenched tight. "Being here could be very bad for Cara's reputation."

"Any worse than being a no-show?" Ethan's eyebrows raised. "I'm her friend, Mr. Byrne. She stood with me when I needed a friend, and I intend to return the favor." He pinned the older man with his stare.

"And it's not as if I was engaged, Dad. I hadn't said yes."

There was really no need to get that in, and Cara felt her face heat as everyone focused their gazes on her. But she hadn't agreed to marry Michael. And although she'd been upset when she heard the news, it was more the upset of being taken for a fool, rather than the soul-wrenching betrayal of being cheated on by a lover.

She'd known down deep inside that Michael wasn't the one. If he had been, she would have had no hesitation in tying herself to him forever. His proposal would have filled her with happiness, rather than the worry and feeling of dread that had coursed through her with his proposal.

"You don't need to put a brave face on it, love," Bill said.

"I'm not."

The faces watching hers were painted with disbelief. Even Ethan.

Maggie waved from across the room.

"Right, we're on." Ethan took her hand.

Cara turned to her parents. "I'll talk to you tomorrow." She really shouldn't feel such relief as walking away from their sympathetic faces. Curse Michael for painting her as a heartbroken ninny!

"You know, if you don't smile, everyone will think I'm a complete bastard," Ethan whispered in her ear. "And I can't afford that in this town, so you better cheer up."

On impulse, she kissed his cheek. She smiled her best Hollywood grin. "We can't have that." She might be a mess of confused emotions inside, but this was Ethan's homecoming. There was no way she was stealing the limelight or tinting this golden evening grey. Not for a moment.

He'd been so generous, bringing the world premiere of the second Crash Carrigan movie to Donabridge. The money they'd raised so far would ensure the future of the twenty-four hour emergency ambulance service the town so vitally needed. He had a personal reason for making sure the ambulance was always there, and he'd worked hard to support all their efforts. She'd make sure everyone knew she was having a good time in his company.

Her lips still tingled with the remembered feel of Ethan's cheek, and her fingers curled around his as they walked through the foyer to the cinema's interior.

ETHAN TUGGED at the gold cufflinks at his wrist. Smoothed a hand over the front button of his suit, and reached for the microphone. Before he even opened his mouth, the chatter died, and all eyes turned to him.

For the first time in years his mouth dried in the spotlight of all that rapt attention. It must be being back here, talking in front of so many people who had known him when he was a teenager.

"I'd like to thank everyone for turning out to see 'Disaster Strikes,'" he said. "And I'd like to thank Fiesta Films for allowing me to contribute to the Donabridge Ambulance Project by holding the premiere here in Donabridge." He stared out into the dimness, not really able to make out any individual faces in the crowd. "As many of you know, my parents died a few years ago in a tragic accident. If the ambulance service had run on a twenty-four hour basis, they might well be alive today. So I understand how vital this service is to the town, and I'm happy to do all I can to ensure that it thrives."

He reached into his inner jacket pocket. "I'm currently filming the third Crash Carrigan film, and I have to return to the set in America tomorrow. Before I left, my director, John Mosse, handed me this." He pulled a sliver of paper out and held it aloft. "It's a contribution from Fiesta Films. A very generous $50,000 contribution."

His words were followed by immediate applause. Ethan stepped forward and handed the check to the head of the organizing committee who was seated on the front row.

He held his hands up, palms front. The buzz of discussion and clapping ceased. "Now, let's watch the movie. Ladies and gentlemen—Disaster Strikes!"

The next two hours dragged. Ethan couldn't bear to watch himself on screen. Every move his screen image made, he could have improved on. Every line delivered on celluloid should have been given a different inflection. And when he stripped off his clothes onscreen and tumbled into bed with his co-star, the silence in the cinema was charged with excitement. He rubbed his chin, looked at the floor, and thanked God that the lights were out.

"Whew!" Cara blew out a breath. "That's scorching acting. Hot Stuff," she whispered.

He could hear the smile in her voice. Somehow her teasing eased his awkwardness. "Somebody's got to do it," he leaned close to whisper in her ear.

He saw her teeth gleam in the reflected light from the giant screen as she smiled.

The theme music picked up. Ethan returned his gaze to the screen. The huge car chase so expertly done by a team of stuntmen was about to start. He relaxed back into the velvet seat and surrendered to fantasy.

At the end of the movie, he and Cara climbed into the limo.

Maggie climbed in too. "I need to talk to you about a few things." She shot a quick glance at Cara.

"Go ahead," Ethan said. There was nothing she couldn't say in front of Cara.

"I have a few messages to pass on. From your co-star and others." Her eyes narrowed. Obviously she thought Cara was his lady for the night rather than just a friend.

Ethan blew out a breath. "Maggie. Cara and I are old friends. That's all. There's nothing you need to be discreet about. Now pass on the messages."

Maggie's mouth tightened. "Okay." The 'you asked for it' remained unsaid, but was evident in her tone. "Alison Bonne rang to thank you for the flowers, and says she hopes to see you on Thursday night. Belle Masterson wanted to know what time your flight was getting in, and Krista—"

"Hold it." Ethan held up a hand. "Was Krista upset?"

Maggie nodded. "Very."

"And rude?"

"X-rated."

"Okay, well I don't think you need to repeat her message. Just forward it to my cell and I'll deal with it when I'm back in the States."

"Right." Maggie clicked a button on her cell, and stowed it in her tiny silver evening bag. She crossed her legs and eyed him expectantly.

Ethan mentally blocked out Cara's silent presence on the seat next to him, and focused on business. "I've packed everything. You'll organize the pick-up from the hotel?"

Maggie nodded. "Yes, on it. The flight is at six, so we'll need to be on the way to the airport at three."

The car slowed at the hotel's entrance.

"Is that it?" Ethan asked.

"Yes, that'll do. I'll see you later." Maggie

climbed out of the car and disappeared into the hotel.

Cara has been so quiet in the quick journey from cinema to hotel—hopefully she wasn't still upset about Michael's desertion.

Ethan leaned close, breathing in the captivating scent of her perfume. It smelled of flowers, with a note of musk. Light, but with dangerous undertones, rather like its wearer. "Okay?" Ethan asked.

Her face was pale, and her hair haloed her head in golden waves. A dimple creased her cheek as she smiled. "You're juggling."

"Women?" He didn't really need to ask. He'd always known what she meant. They'd talked in unfinished sentences since their teens.

"*Lots* of women," Cara said.

"A few women," Ethan corrected. He was faithful to whomever he was seeing—and demanded the same from his bed partners. His co-star Krista Fortuna wasn't quite so disciplined. He'd sent her a diamond bracelet, and terminated their relationship on discovering she was also dating a ballet dancer. Unfortunately Krista wasn't altogether happy with the arrangement.

And Alison and Belle—well, he'd taken then both out to dinner, but hadn't moved any further than a brief kiss goodnight with either. But that was his business.

The car door was open.

"Let's go."

THE LARGE BALLROOM of the Diagio Hotel was ringed with circular tables. Cara was aware of curious glances cast her direction, but at least sitting next to Ethan she didn't have to listen to the whispers, or explain Michael's absence.

She picked up her champagne flute, and sipped. He'd been right—boycotting the event would have caused much more gossip.

The band began to play.

Couples took to the dance floor, swirling to the catchy beat.

Glancing around, Cara noticed Caitlin Murphy stand and smooth down her short skirt over her thighs. She looked at Ethan, swiped her tongue over her upper lip, and stepped forward on heels so high she deserved a round of applause for even attempting it.

Her hips swung outward with each step. Her gaze never left Ethan's face, although he was yet to notice her.

"Dance with me," Ethan's deep voice broke

through Cara's absorbed study of Caitlin's approach. His hand covered hers.

"Maybe later, I think someone else—" Cara broke off as Caitlin reached the table.

Caitlin cleared her throat, cast Cara her *introduce me and I'll be your friend for life* shaky smile.

"Ethan, you remember Caitlin Murphy, don't you? From school?"

Ethan blinked slowly. He obviously didn't remember.

He smiled. "Of course."

Caitlin's face flushed red. Cara saw her knees wobble. Wow, talk about a lady-killer.

"I wondered..." Caitlin swallowed. "I wondered if you might like to..."

"To dance?" Ethan asked. To Cara's relief he didn't leave the question hanging in the air awaiting a response, but instantly answered it. "I'd love to." He squeezed Cara's hand, then pushed back his chair and led Caitlin onto the dance floor.

She tried not to watch them. Tried to drag her eyes away from the way Ethan's hand rested on Caitlin's hip. The way his shoulders moved. He pushed his hair back. When he angled his head down to listen to something Caitlin said, warmth pooled low in Cara's stomach.

Attraction.

Attraction like she'd never felt for Ethan before, in all the years they'd been friends. She wrung the napkin lying on her lap into a twisted rope. He'd always been gorgeous, of course. But somehow she'd never seen him as a man before. He'd always been her friend. Strong, reliable and caring, rather than sexy, dangerous and available.

She brought her glass to her lips, then, realizing it was empty, placed it back on the table again.

It must be because of all the fizzing estrogen in the air. That, and the fact that Ethan was obviously so in demand that she'd have to be deaf, dumb and blind not to notice that every woman in the room was lusting after him. It must be catching.

But when he pulled me out of the costume... Cara clenched her jaw tight and forced the traitorous little voice out of her head. Sure, she'd felt something. Who wouldn't? But Ethan didn't do serious. And having a fling with him would damage their relationship forever.

He was too valuable a friend to fall in love with.

The music faded into silence.

Cara shook out her napkin. Folded it lengthways, then widthways. Smoothed a hand over the creases. Then carefully placed it on the table slightly offset from center. Anything to avoid watching Ethan and Caitlin dancing.

"Right. Your turn." She jumped at Ethan's voice

next to her. "Do *not* turn me down," he said with a determined light in his eye. "I only managed to get away by saying I'd promised to dance with you next."

"Well in that case." She could do this. She wasn't a child. And she'd danced with Ethan loads of times. With any luck, it would be a fast one, and they could keep contact at a minimum.

He led her onto the dance floor.

Pulled her into his arms in time with the slow, saxophone slide.

Her chest was against his, and her nipples tightened under her silk and lace bra. His hand rested on the lower curve of her back. She felt the heat of his palm through the soft purple fabric. His jaw, inches from his mouth, rested against her temple. One hand clasped hers, holding it close to his chest. Cara flattened her other hand against his lapel.

They stepped together in perfect time.

Cara closed her eyes, and let the slow love song wash over her. She breathed in Ethan's familiar smell. His fingers tightened on hers, and his other hand edged her closer.

If she slipped her hand to his hair, angled her face toward his...

A shiver ran through her. She swallowed and pulled out of Ethan's arms. "Sorry, I just have to..."

She glanced to the exit. "I have to go to the ladies room. I'll be back in a moment."

The plaintive love song chased her from the room. She didn't look back.

She'd never run away from anything in her life. But the when the alternative was kissing Ethan, she couldn't run fast enough.

FIVE

Ethan moved his hand over Dee Macey's naked hip, and pulled her on top of him. He stroked a finger across her jaw line. Gazed at her full lips. "You're one hell of a woman." His lips slanted over hers in a kiss.

"Cut! Take five, everybody."

Dee slid off his body, wrapping herself instantly in the open robe held ready by her assistant.

The director, John Mosse, walked over. "Can I have a word, Ethan?"

He glanced away as Ethan slipped into a robe. There was precious little privacy on set. And even though Ethan was not completely naked, filming the steamy love scene, he appreciated John's politeness in averting his eyes.

"How did it go in Ireland?" John asked.

"It went well. They were very appreciative of your check," Ethan said.

"Long flight." John fixed him with a stare. "You must be very tired."

"It was a long flight," Ethan admitted. He knew what John wasn't saying. That his love scene with Dee was lacking in passion.

"Well, here's the thing..."

"I know, John. The love scene stinks." Ethan ran a hand through his hair. Frustration kicked hard in his stomach. Dee Macey was one of the most beautiful women in the world. He sure should be able to at least act as though having her golden flesh sliding against his was arousing. But as he'd held her close, he couldn't help but notice the lack of chemistry between them. There was no tingle as his hand slipped over her golden skin. No frisson as their lips met.

There didn't need to be, of course. He was an actor, not Casanova. But the indifference that he felt for an attractive woman was new.

Maggie had forwarded the messages she'd received while they were in Ireland to his cell phone, and he'd called Alison and cancelled Thursday night's date, saying he was tired after the trip. The truth was that he couldn't get Cara out of his head—much as he tried.

"Take a break, Ethan. Have some coffee, go for a walk; we'll shoot again in ten," John said. "Love scenes can be difficult. You just need to relax, forget we're all here, and focus on making it look as sexy as possible."

Ten minutes later, Ethan lay on the bed and pulled Dee on top of him again. He stroked a finger over her jaw line. Stared at her full lips and imagined an unpainted pair with a soft bow in the top lip. "You're one hell of a woman."

Ethan deliberately infused his gaze with the requisite amount of smolder, angled his head for the perfect camera angle, and kissed her.

It was going to be a long day.

THREE LITTLE WORDS meandered through Cara's mind as she woke. *The morning after.* The horrors of yesterday were over. Today was bound to be a better day.

After all, there was no work to go to, no urgent demands on her time. The best thing about working in a secondary school in Ireland was the three months of holiday every summer.

Cara stretched her arms over her head, and gazed out at the sliver of blue sky visible through the gap in her new cream curtains. It was a new day. A new start. And despite the trauma of the day before, she was strangely at peace with her new reality.

Now that Michael has erased himself so thoroughly from her future, the nagging feeling of indecision clouding her mind had burned off like mist under the heat of the sun.

The long, lazy days of summer stretched out before her.

The past few months had been hectic. Her job in the secondary school was a challenge, and it had taken long months to gain the respect of her class of fifteen-year-old boys. Moving from home for the first time had been hard work too.

Her grandmother's cottage had been run-down and unlivable in when she'd begged her parents to let her renovate it. She'd painstakingly stripped the old wallpaper from the walls, sanded the floors, and organized every aspect of its renovation in the scant hours she had free from marking books, and setting assignments.

Now it was finished.

And the long, lazy days of summer stretched before her with nothing to fill them.

She closed her eyes. Listened to the trilling of a bird outside the window.

A new sound swelled—an approaching car's engine. She waited for it to fade, but instead the throaty roar grew louder as the car turned into her driveway. Then faded into silence. A moment later, the doorbell rang.

Cara glanced at her alarm clock. Nine-thirty. Normally she'd be half way through her first class. She should be up anyway. She climbed out of bed, pulled her dressing gown on, and went to let whoever it was in.

Her brother Ryan stood on the doorstep, clutching a newspaper.

"Hi, Ry..." Cara's eyes widened at his frown.

He stepped and closed the door behind him without a word.

"What's the matter?" she asked.

Ryan was quiet at the best of times, but was completely silent as he walked into the kitchen.

"Ryan!" Cara caught up with him, and grabbed onto his arm. "Don't give me the silent treatment, you know it drives me crazy!"

"You haven't seen the paper then." Ryan threw the local newspaper down on the pine kitchen table.

Two photos covered the front page, under a large banner headline. 'Crash Carrigan in Donabridge!' In the first picture, Ethan's fist connected with Michael's jaw.

Cara reached for the newspaper.

In the picture below it, the photographer had

managed to capture the moment when Ethan pulled her out of the Winnie The Pooh costume, although clever camera angles and editing had removed all evidence of the costume from the zoomed up photo. Her arm was around Ethan's neck. His face was turned in to her throat in what looked like a passionate clinch. Her bra-clad chest was plastered against Ethan, and his hand cupped her bottom.

Cara's hand flew to her mouth. "Oh!"

The caption under the second photo read, 'Local Teacher in X-rated Embrace with Movie Star.'

Cara's knees wobbled. She sank down quickly on a chair.

"What the hell were you doing, Cara?" Ryan's thunderous expression showed he obviously hadn't been talking to their parents. "Michael has asked you to marry him, and you're getting your picture taken snogging bloody Ethan?" He strode from one side of the tiny kitchen to another. "In your underwear!" He stopped and glared. "What on earth..."

Cara stood up and crossed her arms. "Just you wait a minute, Ryan Byrne."

Anger bubbled under the surface as she stared up at her older brother. She extended one arm, and pointed to a chair. "Stop looming over me and sit down."

Ryan's eyes narrowed. He pulled in a breath. Then with a half muttered growl, he jerked the chair from the table and sat down.

"Now don't interrupt."

Ryan's mouth opened. He glowered, then closed it again.

"In this first picture." She slapped the newspaper on the table, and turned it around to face her brother. "Rather than..." she read the caption aloud. "'Ethan Quinn eliminates the competition,' this should read, 'Ethan Quinn stands up for a friend.'" She pushed back the hair that fell into her face, wishing she'd taken the time to tie it before she'd answered the door.

She pulled out a chair and sank into it before her wobbly legs gave out. "Ethan was having a drink with Sean when he saw Michael kissing another woman," she said in a quiet voice. "He..." she gazed down at the photo. "Well, you can see what he did." Her gaze flicked up to Ryan's. "He was protecting me. Being the friend he'd always been." She pulled in a ragged breath. "The papers..."

"And this one?" Ryan's index finger jabbed at the photograph of Cara and Ethan glued together. "It doesn't look innocent, Cara."

"I was stuck inside a costume at the fair, and Ethan pulled me out."

Her brother's eyebrows rose. His expression said what his voice didn't—that he didn't believe her for one moment.

"I know!" She ran her knuckles over her jaw line, feeling the buzz of frustration eat at her insides. "It sounds ridiculous, but I was stuck in a Winnie The Pooh costume."

Ryan blew air out through compressed lips in an audible scoffing sound.

"I was, Ry." Cara frowned. "And it was so hot in there, I'd stripped to my underwear before climbing in. If he hadn't got me out..."

"There are more photos inside." Ryan flicked the pages to the middle.

Cara and Ethan, hand in hand on the red carpet. Her eyes shining, and her warm, intimate smile directed at him. Cara and Ethan in the cinema foyer, his arm around her waist, and his head close to hers as though whispering endearments.

Her parents had been standing directly in front of them both, but the camera angle didn't show them. Despite the innocence of the situation she couldn't help the clutch of reaction as she looked at Ethan's image. He looked so caring. So involved. So, attracted.

They looked like a couple. In lust, if not in love. And the words that accompanied the photographs certainly seemed to be expanding on that theme.

Cara screwed her eyes tight.

"The chief handed it to me the moment I turned up this morning." Ryan's hand covered hers. "It's the talk of the fire station. Which means it's the talk of the town."

Any hint of scandal could affect her job. She'd have to get the paper to print a retraction. Print the truth. Icy dread filled her gut. But to do that, she'd have to reveal that Michael was out with another woman. That even though he'd proposed to her, he wanted to sleep with someone else. That she wasn't enough.

She looked at the picture of Ethan's face so close to her own.

She could deny the fact that she was attracted to Ethan Quinn 'til the cows came home. But no one would believe her. She couldn't blame them. Not with the evidence in print before her very eyes.

"It's not what it looks like, Ry."

It was important that her brother believed her. His approval always had mattered. When her father brought her home from the garda station, Ryan, his mop of black hair every which way, had stumbled down the stairs and silenced her father's harsh reproaches. She'd never forgotten the feel of his warm hand on her shoulder as he stood shoulder to shoulder with her. He'd told her parents that her drink must have been spiked. And the faith in his eyes as he helped her upstairs had brought tears to her own.

"It looks like you care for him," Ryan said quietly.

"Well..." There was no denying it. "I do. He's always been a dear friend to me, you know that."

Ryan nodded. "But people won't believe that's all he is. Not when they see these." He pointed at the photographs. "You look *involved*."

The niggle of disquiet in Cara's stomach solidified into a rock of fear. She had a job, a life. She couldn't let that be in jeopardy, just because she'd accepted her best friend's help when she so desperately needed it.

She pulled her wrap tight.

"I'll call the headmaster to make an appointment to talk to him."

Surely if she explained the situation this could all be sorted out. It was a storm in a teacup that would blow over long before school started again. She'd proved herself able to do the job, and had banished scandal from her life once before, she could do it again.

She saw Ryan to the door.

And wondered if later she should call Ethan.

SIX

Two cars were parked outside the Donabridge School for boys as Cara's mini slid into the parking lot. She picked her handbag off the passenger seat, cast a quick, final look at her reflection in the driver's mirror, and climbed out. She'd dressed in her professional work pantsuit, and spent time straightening her hair to make the best possible impression.

Everyone knew the tabloids weren't to be trusted, didn't they?

Butterflies fluttered in her stomach. She'd worked so hard to get this job. As a newly qualified teacher, she'd been lucky to get it, especially in the current climate where there was such competition for every job going.

The heavy wooden door creaked as it yielded at her push. Then swung back with a whoosh, audible in the still silence of the empty hallway. Cara breathed in the scent of polish and stale air and started walking. High heels clicking on the smooth wooden floorboards.

Shadowy figures were visible through the frosted glass door of the headmaster's office, and the muted murmur of conversation could just be made out in the moment before she knocked.

"Come in," the headmaster's voice called.

Cara pulled in a deep breath, and obeyed.

The headmaster, Mr. Mahon, stood from his mahogany desk as she entered, as did the head of the board of management, Father Delany.

Somehow her feet carried her as far as the desk. A new appreciation of students sent to the head to be reprimanded for causing trouble filled her. "Good afternoon," she said, pleased that at least her voice sounded calm and cool.

All three took their seats.

The newspaper lay on the desk between them, a silent, damning indictment.

"Cara," Mr. Mahon began. "Thank you for coming." His smile faltered and died.

She'd been the one to call for the meeting. So she really shouldn't feel like a naughty schoolgirl, but faced with the grim faces of the two people who could dictate her future, she couldn't help the nerves that had her smoothing nervous hands over her thighs.

"Father Delany and I have spoken to the other members of the board," Mr. Mahon said. "These photographs..." His voice trailed into silence.

His expression sent a flight of butterflies wild in her stomach. Cara clenched her hands in her lap. "These photographs tell a completely false story," Cara said. "Ethan Quinn is an old friend who the papers have tried to insinuate is something more. The first photograph..."

"Where's he's assaulting a local man?" Father Delany interrupted.

Cara nodded. "He was defending my honor, Father. Michael had asked me to marry him, a fact I'd shared with Ethan. So when Ethan saw Michael in the nightclub with another woman..." She swallowed.

Father Delany's eyes widened.

Cara struggled to continue. "Ethan behaved as a friend would. As either of my *brothers* would have."

Mr. Mahon pointed to the second picture. "Yet he appears anything but brotherly in this second picture." His mouth pursed in obvious disapproval. "And your lack of clothing..."

Father Delany's grey head bobbed up and

down. "This is the picture that causes us most problem, Cara. A teacher, barely clothed on the front of the newspaper, in such a compromising position..." His face reddened. "Well, it brings the school into disrepute."

She could tell them about the costume, but the look of disapproval on both faces stilled her tongue. Somehow, before she'd even had a chance to fight her corner, the bout was lost.

"I'm sorry, Cara." Finality rang in Mr. Mahon's tone. "You've been an asset to the school this far, your love of books and your ability to teach isn't in question. However, as a teacher, especially in a boy's school, your ability to do the job has been seriously compromised by this photograph. We've already had a number of telephone calls this morning from parents."

"I can explain," Cara started, in a last ditch attempt to save her job.

"I'm sure you can, dear," Father Delany said, although his expression revealed that he'd be unlikely to believe any words that came from her mouth. "But the board's mind is made up on this matter. I'm afraid we have to terminate your employment."

THE DIRECTOR SHOUTED, "CUT!"

Ethan held onto the rope as the crane slowly lowered him to ground. He stood patiently as the head of the stunt team unstrapped the hidden body harness, and pulled it off.

John Mosse strode over. "That was a good take, Ethan. We don't need to do it again."

Ethan's shoulders relaxed. He felt relief paint a grin on his face. "That's great, John." His face was smeared with fake blood, which itched like the devil. The prosthetic wound that half closed his eye had been irritating him all morning, and his back ached from being suspended over the skyscraper mock-up for the past three hours.

"Half an hour's break, then we'll move on to the shoot-out scene."

"So I'll have to stay in makeup?"

"No, you can clean up. You'll be in SWAT gear," John said. "Makeup will take your scars off now."

If only taking real scars off was as easy as surrendering to the makeup team.

At least Ethan's scars weren't on the surface. He needed his face for his work.

He strode stiff-legged to the makeup trailer. Being back in Ireland had brought the past back into focus. And raising money for the ambulance service had re-opened the old wounds that he and Sean had tried to let grow over. The wound of their mother not reaching the hospital in time to save her life, after the car his father was driving veered off the road and collided with a tree. Their father had been killed instantly, but his mother could have been saved if an ambulance had reached her in time. And if he'd been there, instead of being away, working on a film, maybe the whole damn disaster could have been avoided.

In the makeup trailer, Ethan sat patiently as the makeup lady removed the slivers of rubber from his face. But when Doris approached with a jar of cold cream, he shook his head.

"Just give me some on a hank of cotton-wool, will you, Doris?" I'll take it off in my trailer."

Doris smeared some cold cream onto cotton-wool, and handed it over. "Are you sure, lovey? I can..."

"I'm exhausted. I need to lie down." His voice was harsher than intended, so he softened his words with a smile. "I've been hanging around for hours."

Doris grinned. "I know, we were all watching. It was very exciting. That scene will be dynamite in the movie." The older woman's eyes lit with concern. "Would you like me to get someone to bring you a cuppa? You're looking peaky."

Ethan pulled himself out of the swivel chair,

feeling the burn ache of abused muscles in his thighs. “I’ll be fine, Doris.”

He made it halfway across the lot to his trailer before Maggie caught up with him.

Her skyscraper heels clattered on the asphalt. She was almost jogging—tight pencil skirt gluing her thighs tight together while her calves scissored in rapid motion. He’d told her often enough she didn’t need to dress so fancy while they were on set —she looked completely out of place next to the production assistants and assistant directors strolling around in cargo pants and lace-up boots. But she’d sternly told him she needed to look the part of a Hollywood star’s assistant. She was representing *him* after all.

He’d often thought it was much more likely that she wanted to look like a woman to meet his fellow stars, especially the unattached male ones. He couldn’t really blame her for that. She worked hard. And, by all accounts, played hard too.

He slowed. “Hi, Maggie.”

She gripped a cup of something steaming in a polystyrene cup. The other hand clutched her android phone. As she reached him, she handed over the cup. “Tea. Just the way you like it.”

Ethan accepted it gratefully, and ripped off the top.

“You’re trending on twitter.”

Crash Carrigan was often trending on twitter. It sure didn't merit the look of horror on her face. "Let's talk inside." If he didn't sit ...

Maggie's lips pursed in a thin, you're-not-going-to-like-this line. She trotted along next to him.

Ethan lowered himself into the leather armchair in his trailer, and stuffed a cushion behind his back. "So..." he started.

"It's about Ireland." Maggie slumped onto the cot next to him. "And you're not going to like it." She chewed on her bottom lip.

She actually looked worried. In the five years she'd worked with him, he'd never seen Maggie looked worried before. Annoyed and frustrated, but never worried.

"They've even started a hashtag, and one of those annoying couples word smash-ups."

A dull ache bloomed in Ethan's temples. "What are you talking about?"

"Carethan. It's a combination of Cara and Ethan. It's everywhere."

"Ca..."

"Ca-rethan," Maggie said, stretching the sound out. "Someone got pictures of you and Cara at the event, and they've also dug up pictures of you and Cara, uh..." She blushed. "Well, with her in her underwear."

"What?"

"They also found a picture of you hitting her fiancé." Maggie avoided his eyes. As if somehow thumping that lying dog of an almost fiancé was the greatest of crimes.

"She wasn't engaged," he snapped.

Maggie's gaze flicked to his.

"He'd proposed, but she hadn't accepted." He reached over and took the cell phone from her hand, and scrolled through the ever growing list of tweets with #carethan before them.

"My phone's been ringing every second with journalists wanting a quote. I don't know what to tell them."

The paparazzi were relentless, chasing something like this. If they tracked Cara down...Ethan's blood ran cold in his veins. Maybe they already had. "Who published the photos?"

Maggie's brow creased. "I can't remember the name, it was a paper in Ireland." She pushed back the sleeve of her tight black jacket and looked at her watch. "You will be wanted in wardrobe soon."

They needed damage limitation. Fast. Adrenalin flooded Ethan's veins. "Track down a copy of the paper online. I need to see the pictures and what they're saying." He drained his tea. "I need to make a phone call."

As the trailer door closed behind Maggie, Ethan punched in Cara's number. It rang for a few moments, then he heard her familiar voice.

"Ethan?"

Relief flooded him. "Cara. I heard about the newspaper."

"It's been crazy here." Fatigue flattened her voice. "I've had one hell of a day. The school..."

Damn, he hadn't even thought about her job. Having your teacher plastered all over the front of the paper in their underwear would be every schoolboy's dream, and every teacher's nightmare. "What happened?" He reckoned he knew the answer to the question before he asked it, but asked anyway. His hand clenched into a fist. If only he was there, he could offer her some sort of comfort.

A G-rated vision of sliding an arm around Cara's shoulders, pulling her body close to offer comfort suddenly went right to NC-17 with the thought of pressing his lips against hers, sliding his hand down her back...

"They sacked me." Her quiet voice jerked him back to reality.

Ethan closed his eyes.

"I won't get another job as a teacher. Not now."

The entire situation was beyond unfair. She'd been so happy when she'd got the job. It gave her the funds to finally strike out from her family to make a home for herself. They'd burned up the wires for nights on end, her telling him of the improvements she'd made to her grandmother's cottage.

Once the paparazzi tracked her down things would only get worse.

"Come out to stay with me." The words were out before his brain kicked in. If she arrived in America, the press would be more focused on their relationship, not less. But he couldn't just leave her to the jaws of the rabid press.

He winced at her brittle laugh.

"Ah, Ethan." Her voice warmed with a hint of the old Cara. "That's sweet, but..."

"But nothing." He was responsible for destroying her career. What did she have to lose by spending time with him anyway? At least if she was in his new place in Malibu the press wouldn't be able to hound her, the estate had been specially chosen because of its high walls and strictly enforced privacy. "I've just bought a house in Malibu. I haven't moved in properly yet, I've been waiting for the movie to be finished. You can help me get settled in. I need you, Cara."

The idea was perfect. There was less than a week more of filming to complete. They could hang out, talk about old times. Brainstorm ideas to get her back on her feet.

"You're feeling sorry for me, Ethan," Cara's voice was low and quiet. "I appreciate that, really. But I don't need you to. It'll all die down in a day or so."

Ethan stood to pace the trailer. "You don't know the half of it. The internet is buzzing with the story. It's gone global. Things are only going to hot up from here on in."

"It's a non-story," Cara insisted. "Once we both tell them that we're just friends—"

"Just friends?" Ethan ran a hand through his hair and held back a groan. "Have you any idea how often celebrities insist they're just friends, Cara? Just friends means there's a hot and heavy affair going on. They won't let it go. If you're here, at least I can protect you until some other scandal hits the tabloids."

He rubbed the ache blooming at his temples. Now they'd got their very own couple-tag, it would be practically impossible for the press to let it go. But at least if they were together they could work something out. Maybe even pretend to be in love, and then have a public break-up. "I'll organize a ticket and email it to you."

"Don't." Cara's voice was laced with determination. "Honestly, Ethan. I know you want to protect me, but I'm not a child. I don't...to be looked after." She must be walking around—the signal was dropping mid-sentence. "My dinner is burning. I'll...tomorrow."

Before he had a chance to respond, she was gone–her voice replaced by dead air.

SEVEN

Life changes in a split second. When the path that you're following disappears, there are two things you can do. Stop dead, or search in the undergrowth for another route. Cara smothered jam on her morning croissant, and considered her options. When Ethan suggested a visit to America, she hadn't for one moment considered it.

He'd stepped onto the path to his future years ago, when he'd left Donabridge at seventeen to enroll in acting school in Dublin. His mother had been the driving force in helping him achieve his dream, and worked two jobs to pay the fees.

All her sacrifices paid off the moment he got his first role in a celebrity-heavy movie filming in

Dublin. Even as a bit-actor, he'd commanded the screen, and his Hollywood debut had come soon after.

Unlike Ethan, she'd struggled to find a niche to settle in. Her love of writing and the written word had been the reason she went to college to get her English degree. But an English degree wasn't worth much in the currency of getting-a-job, so she'd followed it up with a teacher training course.

Now that dream was over, the future was clouded. At least she had the cottage rent free, but she'd need something to support herself. What that something might be eluded her.

Cara swallowed a mouthful of coffee. The blows had come so quickly she still reeled from them. Mere days ago, she'd been considering whether she should accept Michael's proposal. Looking forward to introducing her students to Shakespeare. Now all that was yesterday's news.

Just, hopefully, as she was.

She picked up the gift voucher that Ryan had given her for her birthday and pushed back the kitchen chair. She'd booked a facial and eyelash dye for today a week ago. Maybe being slathered in goo and relaxing while someone fussed over her would restore her spirits. It certainly couldn't hurt.

An hour later, lying on the padded couch in

'Temptations' with her eyes glued together with black dye, and her face covered in a lavender scented mask, Cara listened to the discordant clanging of the oriental 'relaxation' music and tried to stop her racing mind. She hated having her eyelashes dyed.

"Don't open your eyes. I'll be back in ten minutes," the beautician said, instantly filling Cara with the compulsion to flicker her eyelids open, despite the cold paste covering her lashes.

"Right," she managed.

"Relax," the disembodied voice advised, tucking a warm blanket around her.

The sound of a match striking was followed by the musky scent of a joss stick, doubtless more 'atmosphere.'

Cara's nose twitched. She only had to bear it for ten minutes. She'd be able to open her eyes soon...

A door slammed in the outer room.

"You can't go in there!" the beautician's familiar voice warned.

A cool breeze chilled the mixture on Cara's face. "Cara Byrne?" a soft female voice with a British accent asked.

"Who..."

"I'm sorry, Miss Byrne. I told this woman you couldn't be disturbed," the beautician said. "You'll have to come back. She's half way through her treatment."

"I just have a few questions."

Cara's hands clenched into fists. She fought the instinct to open her eyes, and possibly destroy her vision forever. "I don't know who you are, but I'm hardly in a position to talk to you at the moment," she forced through gritted teeth. "Leave me alone please."

"My readers would like to know about you and Ethan Quinn," the voice continued. "If you could just give me a quote..."

"You want a quote?" Cara felt her blood heat. She was stuck under a blanket, with her face covered with goo, and her eyes iced together. She couldn't stand up and push the intruder from the room, and the beautician had gone suspiciously quiet, maybe she was agog to hear the quote too. "I'll give you a quote. Bugger off."

Silence. Followed by the slamming of one door, then another.

"I'll take the dye off now," the beautician whispered.

"You might as well take the mask off too." No way she staying here one moment longer than necessary.

She felt the characteristic cold slide of water-soaked cotton wool chill her eyelid.

"Did she say who she was?" Cara asked.

Another swipe of cold cotton wool on the other eye.

"She just pushed in here. Didn't say anything apart from what she said to you. She had one of those little tape recorder thingys...I'm so sorry, this has never happened before. I feel so terrible, your entire relaxing facial is ruined." A dry cloth swept over Cara's eyelids. "You can open your eyes now."

Cara's eyes flickered open, and relief flooded her as the room came into focus.

"Okay?" The beautician's face bisected her field of vision.

"Fine." Cara forced a smile. "It wasn't your fault, don't worry about it." The face mask slid on her brow as she frowned. "I wonder how she found me." After all, no one knew of her appointment except her and the salon.

Cara sank back onto the salon bed, and closed her eyes as the beautician wiped off the face mask.

The beautician's blue eyes stared into hers. Her extra-long false eyes fluttered. "I saw her from the window. That mini's yours isn't it?"

Cara nodded, as the wet cloth swiped over her mouth.

"She walked up to it and read the number plate. I guess she must have discovered that was your car."

Which meant she must have done quite a lot of

research to track Cara down. The reporter must know where she lived too.

Perhaps she wasn't yesterday's news after all.

CARA'D TOLD him she didn't need his help. But she had no idea what she was dealing with. By the time filming was finished for the day, Ethan had, with Maggie's help, organized a flight from Dublin to LA for the following morning, and cancelled filming for the following day.

John Mosse hadn't been happy about telling the assembled cast and crew about the change of plans, but when Ethan had agreed to cover all the considerable expenses involved, and the actors and crew had agreed to work an extra day over the weekend (at a considerable bonus rate, also covered by Ethan) he'd reluctantly agreed.

"She must be worth a lot," he said, as Ethan wrote a personal check. "An *awful* lot," he reiterated as he glanced at the amount before stuffing the check in his pocket.

"She is." Ethan's heart clenched at the thought of Cara being hounded by the press. She'd been through so much in the past week; she must be at breaking point.

He climbed into his car and drove to the sterile,

empty condo in West Hollywood that served as a temporary home. He threw his keys on the table, added crushed ice from the refrigerator into a tall glass, and topped it up with fresh orange juice. Then he strode to the phone and called Sean.

"I wondered when I was going to hear from you." His brother's familiar lilt sounded so close he could almost be in the same room. "Things are crazy here."

"Here too." Ethan drank a cold mouthful. "I've emailed you a ticket. I need you to get Cara onto a plane tomorrow morning. I can take care of her here. She won't like it, I talked to her earlier and she told me she could handle it, but..."

"A lot's happened since this morning," Sean said. "Cara drove into the station this afternoon, being chased by a ton of reporters and photographers."

Ethan clamped his teeth together as tension gripped his shoulders. "Is she all right?" Frustration at not being there made his tone sharp. "She shouldn't be alone."

"Calm down, bro. She's fine. We dressed her as a ban-garda and slipped her out of the station without any of them realizing. She's staying with me. Do you want to talk to her?"

Ethan gripped the phone. "Yes."

After a brief moment, Cara's husky tones

sounded in Ethan's ear. "I guess you were right." Her laugh sounded forced. "It's been crazy."

He'd got used to the press's attention, but Cara had no experience of it. Until he'd brought it to her door. Ethan rubbed his eyes. He shouldn't have hit Michael, not in a place where every person had a cell phone with a camera.

"What happened?"

"A journalist ambushed me in the salon when I was covered in a face mask and getting my eyelashes dyed. I told her to bugger off, so that'll probably be in the papers tomorrow morning." She sighed. "Then when I popped into the supermarket on the way home, a photographer stepped up and brazenly took a series of shots of me at the till. Focusing on my shopping basket."

Curiosity piqued, Ethan asked, "What had you bought?"

"Ice cream, black rubbish sacks, and tampons," Cara replied. "God knows what stories they'll get from that."

"At least you hadn't bought a pregnancy test," Ethan said.

"Yes, small mercies." Silence followed her words—stretched for long moments.

"They won't leave until they have a story. I've booked a flight for you tomorrow morning, Sean has the ticket." Ethan said in a tone that brooked no argument. "I'll pick you up at the airport."

"Isn't that just going to add fuel to the flames?"

"Probably, but there's nothing either of us can do to dowse them at this stage. I want you to be close. At my house in Malibu, at least you can avoid being hassled every time you go outside." Suddenly he wanted to see her more than he wanted to take his next breath. Wanted to spend every moment with her. To check for himself that she wasn't hurting by anything he'd done. Wanted to be there for her, in the way she'd been there for him when the Aoife Fitzpatrick, the woman he'd thought himself in love with, had followed him to Hollywood and broken his heart.

The strength of his desire dried his mouth. The memory of Cara's azure eyes staring into his as he'd pulled her close, her chest and firm thighs against his flooded his body with remembered sensation. "I'll see you tomorrow."

Since Aoife, his relationships with women followed a predictable trajectory. Date, bed. Goodbye. Maybe because the women he dated knew Ethan Quinn movie star, rather than Ethan Quinn man. A relationship with Cara would be different. She not only knew his entire history but liked him for who he really was, rather than the faked-up public persona that he lived in Hollywood.

She was the only woman he'd let close. Because there had never been the possibility of involvement between them.

But the sands had shifted.

Having Cara enter his world was going to be dangerous.

EIGHT

There was absolutely no reason why she should have worn her sexiest jeans. Or the top that dipped low in the front. Apart from the fact that she needed every last drop of confidence that looking her best lent her. *Just keep telling yourself that,* Cara thought, pushing out the little voice that mocked she was dressing for Ethan.

In one way, she was. After all, if she was going to be photographed as his current squeeze, she owed it to him to at least look vaguely enticing. *Who are you kidding? You want to see that look in his eyes again...* The look that heated her blood and made her body all tingly when he pulled her close on the dance-floor. The one he'd never directed at her in all the years they'd known each other.

She'd never questioned her feelings for Ethan before. But then, she'd never felt quite like this about him either. Ethan didn't do serious. Never flirted with long-term. A quick fling could ruin their relationship forever. But just the thought of him broke her out in goosebumps. Which *couldn't* be good.

The *fasten seat belts* light went on.

"We'll be landing in the next few moments, please ensure that your tables are in the clipped-up position," a disembodied voice drawled.

Cara shoved her latest read, a compelling biography of a woman prison warder, in her bag and slipped her feet back into the high-heeled sandals. She pulled her hairbrush out of the bag, and quickly reapplied her makeup.

"Meeting someone special?" the elderly lady who'd been her companion in first class for the last twelve hours asked. Appearances could be deceptive. Rather than an old lady visiting family, Juliet was an octogenarian writer whose thriller was going to be turned into a film.

"My friend is meeting me at the airport," Cara said.

"A man friend?" Juliet's eyes twinkled with mischief. Dimples formed perfect dents in her powdery cheeks.

Cara felt her cheeks heat in a flush. "A man friend," Cara confirmed. "How about you?"

"My agent. My book is being made into a film—I have to meet with the scriptwriter and read through his treatment."

"It's so exciting!" Cara leaned closer.

"I never thought I'd see one of my books on the silver screen," Juliet said. "Especially at my age."

"I guess you never know what twists and turns your life will take."

Over the long flight they'd talked about everything. A shared love of writing had formed an unexpected bond, and the enforced proximity had strengthened it.

"Pass me your cell phone." Juliet extended a wrinkled hand with pink painted nails. "I want to put my number into it."

Cara handed it over.

Juliet carefully added Cara's number into her own cell too. After passing it back, Juliet continued. "I'd love to meet you for lunch if you're in central Hollywood. I've enjoyed meeting you."

"Me too, Juliet," Cara said, surprised to realize how true her words were. Juliet's agile mind and quick wit had been a godsend during the flight. She'd confided that she'd lost her job, but hadn't gone into detail about Ethan. Some things weren't meant for sharing. "I'm staying with a friend in

Malibu, so I don't know if I'll be able to join you for lunch, but I'll certainly try."

"Do, honey." Juliet patted her hand in a grandmotherly way. "Oh, and I have something for you." She reached into her bag, and pulled out a book with a gory picture of a man with a slashed throat on the cover, with the title, *Edge of Night*, written below it.

"Yours?" Cara's voice sounded faint. Somehow she'd imagined Juliet's book to be more cozy than slasher.

"Mine." Juliet's head jerked down then up. Pride lit her eyes. "A psychological thriller about a very complex man." She giggled. "You should see your face!"

Cara smiled. "I didn't expect..."

"People never do, dear." Juliet patted her hand. "You should never judge anyone by their appearance, you know. What's inside may surprise you."

The lights dimmed.

"Oh good, we're landing." Juliet clasped her bag on her lap. Leaned closer and whispered into Cara's ear. "Don't worry. This little career break will turn out for the best, you'll see."

The plane dipped toward the runway. Cara stowed her makeup bag and mirror in her bag, pulled in a lungful of air. And prepared to land.

LEANING against a pillar outside the arrivals gate, Ethan glanced at his Rolex. He hadn't managed to escape detection; two girls across the concourse had caught his eye with their excited smiles on the way in.

The first trickle of fresh travelers had walked through a few minutes ago. He searched the wave that followed for her face without success.

Around him, reunited families hugged and laughed. His stomach clenched at their happy faces. In the years since he'd been in California, he'd never greeted anyone at the airport. Never persuaded his last living relative, Sean, to make the trip.

Time seemed to stand still as he waited. The tinny voice announced another flight. Then, pushing a trolley laden with bags, Cara appeared. A diminutive, white haired woman walked alongside her, and the two were deep in conversation.

"Juliet!" A tall, dark haired man waved in Cara's direction and hurried over.

With a smile, the lady introduced the newcomer to Cara, who surrendered the trolley to his care before kissing the lady's cheek.

Cara looked around.

The moment their gazes connected, Ethan felt

as though the air had been forced out of his lungs. Dressed simply in tight, navy jeans and a red T-shirt that showcased every dangerous curve, she was simply stunning.

She smiled.

Ethan struggled for air.

She said something to the lady and her friend—who both glanced in Ethan's direction—and said her goodbyes. "Hey!" she said, walking toward him. "There you are."

Ethan shook the cobwebs out of his brain and took the overnight bag from her shoulder. "Good to see you." His voice sounded gravelly, as though he'd been dragging himself on his stomach through the desert for days without water. He swallowed. "Good flight?"

Somehow, without any prompting from his brain, his body moved closer. She smelled of lemons. His face lowered to hers, and his mouth dusted across her mouth.

She stayed so still she might have been carved from stone.

"Yes, good," she whispered, her breath warming his lips.

The urge to pull her into his arms, to really kiss her, flashed like lightning.

Her pupils expanded into large black pools.

A breathless voice shattered the spell. "Can we have a picture?"

The girls had made it across the concourse and stood close by. He couldn't believe he hadn't registered their approach.

Ethan stepped back. "Sure."

Both girls giggled as he gifted them with his best movie star grin. From the corner of his eye, he saw Cara rub a hand across her eyes as if to obliterate his image.

"Who's first?" He stretched one arm out in silent invitation.

"Oh, we don't want a picture with you, we want a picture of the two of you together," one of the girls explained. "You're Cara, aren't you?"

Cara's jaw dropped. "I..."

"My friend's just come off a long flight," Ethan said. "I'm sure she'd prefer..."

The girl pouted. "Oh, please..."

Ethan glanced around. People seemed to be watching the tableau unfolding before them with interest. They really needed to get out of here as soon as possible.

Cara stepped close, picked up his arm, and draped it over her shoulder. "Yes, I'm Cara." She smiled brightly at the girls. "I don't mind being photographed."

All smiles again, the girls quickly snapped a picture.

"Now, we have to go." With a glance at the doors, Cara efficiently engineered their exit, leaving Ethan free to follow in her wake.

In two long strides, he caught up with her. "Do you even know where you're going?"

She shot him a glance beneath long dark lashes. Her cheek dimpled. "I haven't a clue—I just thought we ought to get out of there before you drew any more attention."

"*We* drew any more attention." Ethan slipped his hand into hers, feeling the familiar jolt as their palms connected. "Those girls were more interested in seeing you than they were seeing me." He pushed the door open.

"Aw." Cara pouted. "Feeling edged out of the spotlight?"

The urge to laugh fought with the urge to kiss her senseless. As they were in public, laughter won.

He pulled her along to the silver Aston-Martin waiting at the curb. "I'll deal with you when we get home." The mere thought of what dealing with her might entail sent his mind spiraling into unfamiliar territory. Or unfamiliar when it came to Cara. An imagined land of very little clothing, and plenty of heat.

Ethan rubbed a hand over his hair. "Buckle up."

"I hope you've got some food ready for me," Cara teased. "You know I'm always hungry."

Hungry for me? Ethan squashed the thought. He'd always been able to tease her without innuendo, why was the first thought that bloomed in his mind such a provocative one? "Yeah, you're a complete greedy guts." The powerful car shifted up a gear as they sped through the traffic.

"Well, I'm not a skinny actress, that's for sure." Was that a note of defiance in her voice.

"I don't know where you put it." He glanced over. "You must have hollow legs."

Cara's laughter filled the car, so infectious he couldn't help laughing too.

"So, rashers, sausages and beans, I reckon," she teased. "Or have your culinary skills improved since you last cooked for me?"

Sunday brunch had been their thing, and he'd always cooked it because Cara was incapable of doing much more than heating a can of soup. Ethan's mind flashed back to the hours they'd spent across the pine table in his mother's kitchen. He'd always made brunch, and she'd always brought the Sunday papers.

The realization hit him that the moments with Cara had been what he'd looked forward to all week, and she'd never let him down. Had been there, rain or shine.

"I've expanded my repertoire," Ethan said.

"Oh, have you?" The teasing tone in her voice hinted at things unspoken. "Well, I guess after so many years..."

"I've grown up." Ethan clutched the steering wheel.

In the years since he left Ireland, he'd had plenty of time to enjoy a different life. Many different women. And from the moment he'd pulled her out of that damned costume, and felt her warm curves, his feelings for Cara had deepened and intensified. There was no way he could deny it to himself any longer. He wanted her with a soul-deep longing that tangled his insides and turned his brain to mush. And try as he might, there was no stuffing that particular genie back in the bottle.

FLIRTING WAS FUN.

And when you knew the person almost as well as you knew yourself, it was darned irresistible. Cara should tell by the glint in Ethan's eye, the way his body shifted on the black leather seat as she laughed, that he was feeling the tug of attraction too.

She gazed out of the window, tilted her head up toward the blue sky, and felt her spirit soar like a bird high above. She could feel the smile on her face, and with another man, might have felt embarrassed to be so goofy, but with Ethan...

"Enjoying yourself?"

"Oh, you have no idea how much." She stretched her arms out in front of her, and rotated her wrists. "Being here is wonderful."

The dark skies and blacker mood that had pressed down on her in Donabridge, had been banished ever since she walked through the doors and saw him lounging against a pillar, waiting for her.

Once, it would have been as natural as breathing to tell him that being with *him* was wonderful. She would have kissed his cheek, or reached for his hand. But the attraction, slow-burning through her core, sending little tingles through her, stilled her voice in her throat. Saying such things meant more, somehow, now.

She hadn't wanted things to change between them. But it had. The moment she'd seen him in Donabridge. And right now there was no way she wanted to turn back the clock. "I like your hair."

Ethan's dark eyebrows rose. "I can't wait to cut it," he growled in a voice so deep that it sent shivers through her. "One more week."

"Will you leave it long—for me? Just until I go." She hadn't given much thought to how long she was staying; the ticket he'd sent was one way. "I'm just going to stay for a couple of weeks. Is that all right, you won't be fed up with me by then?"

"I want you to stay for longer. At least a month," Ethan said. "I need you to help get my house sorted. I'm working all next week, so you'll be alone a lot of the time." He glanced over, and his mouth tilted in a smile so familiar her heart stuttered.

"So, I'll be slaving away while you're out enjoying yourself?"

"That just about covers it. I'm a real slave driver."

A house on the beach, sun, sand, *sex* popped into her mind and she shook her head quickly to dispel it.

"Seriously, Cara. I'm sorry everything has gone so badly. I want you to take some time out. To re-evaluate."

Cara's mood burst like a balloon full of fanciful dreams striking a pin. She'd been fantasizing about a crazy affair while Ethan obviously felt nothing but guilt and pity for his old friend. Sure, he'd flirted, but he was incapable of not flirting, once someone else started it. He'd bedded all his leading ladies, hadn't he?

Her mouth dried. Thank goodness, she hadn't embarrassed herself by throwing herself at him. He was so gallant he'd probably have kissed her too, rather than tell her the truth.

Cara picked her bag off the floor, and made a pretense of searching inside, just so he wouldn't see her lip quivering.

"I can't wait for the film to be over," Ethan continued, staring straight ahead. "I want to move all my stuff out to the beach house. I hate living with half my things in each place. I always want something that's in the other house."

"There must be advantages to filming?" Cara asked. "I mean, you love the acting, right?"

"This is my last Crash Carrigan movie," Ethan said, with a note of finality in his tone. "I don't want to be typecast. As a character, he's sort of one-dimensional. I need more of a challenge."

"Is a different actress playing your love interest?"

She knew the answer, but couldn't resist digging for information about his latest leading lady, a leggy glamazon who, by all accounts, in life had just as voracious an appetite as the characters she portrayed on screen.

"Dee Macey's in this one. She's a good actress." His mouth compressed into a tight line.

"And she's gorgeous," Cara added.

"She knows it too," Ethan said. "But believe me, it's hard work lying on top of her all day."

"Ethan!" Cara's voice came out as a squeak. "I can't believe you said that."

"It's just fact. I spent the last day on set lying in bed with her."

"Kissing?" She tried to keep her mouth from drooping at the corners, rolled her lips in, as her stomach clenched at the thought of Ethan and the glamazon in a clinch.

Ethan puffed out air. "Kissing, pretending to make love, the whole thing." He looked decidedly unhappy about it. "We have lousy chemistry, and it shows. Take after take. It was a nightmare."

A smile warmed her heart, heated her throat, and finally tilted her lips. "Aw. Hard day at the office?"

"Decidedly not hard." Ethan grinned. "Definitely limp."

"You, Ethan Quinn, are a naughty boy."

Ethan slid a warm hand over her knee. "Damn right."

NINE

They drove for miles along the wide highway, beside the azure ocean. Cara cracked the window open, and a warm sea breeze lifted her hair. She could taste a trace of salt on her lips. Being here felt like a new beginning. A new chapter in her life, unopened, unexplored. Unexpected.

The silver Aston-Martin slowed, and the indicator's tick punctuated the silence. As the powerful car turned, ornate silver gates swung open automatically between high stone walls topped with iron railings.

"Home," Ethan murmured as a house came into view.

In this obviously wealthy neighborhood, she'd somehow expected a mansion, but her heart fluttered and soared at the simple wooden beach house surrounded by a romantically overgrown garden. She pulled in a lungful of air. "It's beautiful."

The car slowed, then stopped. In moments, Ethan was at her side, opening the door wide. "Come and look at the other side." His mouth curved in that grin that melted women's hearts, world over. He reached for her hand and tugged.

Bleached wooden steps led from the front of the house steeply down through a swathe of terraces filled with cascading greenery and large succulents. The wooden handrail was hot to Cara's touch, and she concentrated carefully on the way down, as the soft swoosh of the ocean grew louder. Soon, she was standing on a silver beach. The sea lapped against the shoreline, lacy sea-foam caps on the waves breaking up as they sank into the sand.

"Wow." Cara slipped off her shoes and picked them up. The hot sand felt like powdered sugar beneath her soles. Pure, clean, *fabulous*.

"Come on." Ethan walked along the beach behind the beach house.

"It's on stilts," Cara said with wonder in her tone.

"We keep the Zodiak here." Ethan pointed to a launch ramp built in under the house. "I use it sometimes for fishing. "It's fully stocked with loungers and a barbeque."

Cara glanced up. "All that glass would keep a window cleaner busy."

Ethan nodded. "Well, there's not much point to having a view if you can't see it."

"From every room in the house, apparently." Cara itched to see inside, to investigate the rooms beyond the wide balcony that stretched across the entire back of the house. But Ethan sat on the sand, stretching his long legs. He slipped off his shoes, dug his toes into the sand, and sighed.

She dropped next to him.

"So..." Ethan slung an arm over her shoulders. "No one will bother you here. The place is impenetrable." He stared into her eyes. "How are you doing?"

She opened her mouth to speak. His eyes darkened with a warning. "Really. Don't tell me some line. I'll know."

Cara swallowed. "I'm okay."

Ethan's arm tightened. "I'm sorry that bastard broke your heart," he murmured. "I know it had to hurt." A shadow of pain flickered across his eyes, and he stared out to the ocean. His jaw tightened.

"It wasn't the same as you and Aoife," Cara said. "You loved her."

Ethan stayed silent, but he didn't need to

confirm her words. They'd talked through Aoife's desertion on the telephone two years ago. The fact that Aoife had treated him so callously had fired Cara's blood red hot, back then. She'd seemed devoted when she packed in her job as a secretary and set off for a new life with the man everyone had thought she would marry. But she'd been wooed by the glamour of it all, and had her head turned when a bigger movie star turned his considerable charms her direction at a party. And had quickly switched allegiance.

No one except Cara knew just how devastating Aoife's desertion had been.

Cara grasped Ethan's hand, hanging from her shoulder. "Has there been anyone, since?"

"Plenty of anyone's," Ethan's voice was hard. "But no one special."

The murmur of the ocean was a backdrop to his words.

"Michael and I...it wasn't like that." Cara needed to let him know that she wasn't hurting the way he had, back then. "We'd been dating, but..." Her tongue swept over her lips, tasting salt. "I hadn't really committed to the relationship, even after he proposed. Something just didn't seem right." She glanced at his profile. "You know?"

Ethan's gaze tangled with hers. "You went to bed with him. I know you don't do that lightly."

"I didn't." All embarrassment at discussing her love life faded. She'd always told Ethan everything, had only held back from this revelation because she'd been sure he wouldn't understand. Under the circumstances, relief flooded through her at the knowledge that deep-down, some part of her had known Michael wasn't to be trusted with her heart. Or the rest of her body, for that matter.

"You didn't?" Ethan's gaze dipped to focus on her mouth. "What—*never?*"

"Not even a little bit." Cara felt her mouth tilt in a smile. "I guess I knew, somehow."

Ethan leaned close. Touched his lips to hers in a feather-light caress so brief, she almost thought she'd imagined it. "I'm glad," he said in a deep voice, before standing up and holding his hand out to her. "Want to have a look inside?"

ETHAN PONDERED CARA'S words as he opened up the house. Sleeping with someone didn't mean anything. Merely that both parties felt the tug of sexual attraction, and acted on it. But somehow the fact Cara hadn't actually allowed such a level of intimacy with Michael sparked something deep inside.

She wasn't like him. Up until now, she hadn't

done casual. Her innate belief in true love was one of the things that made her Cara. And even as his body responded to her with only one look from those sky-blue eyes, he couldn't—wouldn't—be the one to initiate her into the joys of sex for sex's sake.

She gazed around the large living room. A smile tilted her lips up. "I love it—it's just like being outside."

The large white leather sofas, polished pale pine floorboards, and plain white painted walls echoed the white sand beyond the window. The entire house was designed to showcase the view, not to compete with it. And when the evenings drew in, long white curtains closed the view out, and the focus shifted to the fire he'd light in the huge fireplace. He'd moved in a couple of essentials, like the fifty-inch TV in the corner, and a fluffy sheepskin rug to soften the austerity and add warmth and luxury. And when he finally moved in the rest of his scant possessions, it would feel more like home.

He waved at the desk in the corner. "There's a laptop there, in case you feel like browsing the net, or checking your email."

"The bedrooms are over here." He walked through to the master bedroom as she followed in his wake. "This is mine." He pushed open the door.

"Great bed." Cara walked to the four-poster,

and bounced her bottom on it. "I guess you just lie here and stare out at the sea, huh?" Her eyes lit with a teasing light. "Or are you too busy concentrating on the ladies you bring here?"

"I haven't brought any ladies here." Ethan watched her eyes darken as he sat next to her on the patchwork cover he'd brought from Ireland. "I haven't brought anyone here, actually."

"You mean I'm the first?" Cara asked.

"Yeah." She was the first. The first friend he'd had, as a kid. The first person he confided in. The first woman he wasn't prepared to take to bed. He stood up. "Come on, I'll show you your room."

ETHAN WAS ACTING STRANGE. It had started while they sat on his bed, and continued as he carried her bag in from the car and plonked it on the spare bed. He was avoiding eye contact. Holding part of himself back.

"Why don't you get into your swimming costume and we'll go for a swim?" he asked, shoving his hands in his pockets.

"That sounds great." She bit back the questions that bubbled up inside. What's changed? Why are you being so...so distant? Sometimes, when he was bothered by things, he'd retreat and go silent. This looked like one of those times. She flipped open her suitcase. "Everything okay?"

"Fine." Ethan stepped to the doorway, and stood there for a moment, just looking at her. "I'll go get ready too." He pulled the door closed behind him as he strode from the room.

There was no point dwelling on it. He'd tell her when he wanted to. Or bottle it up inside, and get over it. Nothing she could say or do would speed up the process. She unpacked the turquoise bikini she'd bought in Dublin in preparation for an Irish summer that hadn't materialized. Skimpy shoestring straps, and tiny triangles of fabric.

She sighed. In this, there'd be no hiding the fact that she was considerably curvier than Ethan's regular playmates. And instead of the all-over tan that Californian girls sported, her body was milk white. At least she'd match the beach.

She slipped her clothes off, and put the bikini on. Then wandered to the floor length mirror in a wooden frame that graced a corner of the bedroom. Urgh, even worse than she'd thought. Her breasts swelled above the tiny triangles, although luckily the fabric was thick enough to hide her nipples from view. And the space between the top and bottoms revealed acres of white stomach. She turned sideways. At least her regular gym routine meant that she had abs. She swiveled even further.

Swiped a hand across her bottom as she peeked over her shoulder at her rear view. *No, Cara, your bum doesn't look big in this.* A giggle bubbled up and out as she thought the words.

How ridiculous that she was obsessing over her body. She never had body issues, but somehow being in Malibu had instantly given her some. It must be because at home, she never swanned around in such skimpy outfits.

She snatched a towel from the pile on the chair, and a tube of sun-cream from her suitcase, and slipped into her flip-flops with the huge flower on top that she'd, on impulse, bought at the airport. It couldn't just be the thought of baring her body before Ethan, that would be ridiculous.

She stopped outside his bedroom door. "Ethan?"

No answer. She pushed open the door to see his clothes tossed casually on the bed. A search of the living room revealed he wasn't there either. He must already be on the beach.

She saw him in the water the moment she stepped onto the sand.

With a quick smooth over the string at her hip, she dropped her things on the sand, slipped off the flip-flops and walked to the waterside. Warm waves lapped over her toes. She walked further, up to her ankles.

"Come on in," Ethan called.

Even though he wasn't far from shore, he must be in deep, for the water covered all but his head. He pushed back his wet hair with one tanned hand, and grinned.

The water swirled around her calves, then her knees, and finally enclosed her hips with its soothing caress.

"Watch out for—"

The ground disappeared, and water engulfed her head.

Strong arms slid around her waist, pulling her to the surface.

She spluttered, and shook her head, feeling the water plaster her soaked hair against the side of her face.

"I was trying to tell you to watch out because the ground slopes away." Ethan held her body close against his, treading water to keep them upright.

"*Now* you tell me." Cara rolled her eyes. "You could have mentioned it earlier." She tried to frown, but a smile fought and won.

"The water's nice, though, isn't it?" Ethan's face was close. So close, with one tiny movement she could move her lips against his damp ones. His lean thighs brushed against hers as they moved under the water. Her hands rested on his broad shoulders, her nipples pressed against his wide chest. Their stomachs touched. Below, she felt the insistent press of something hard against her pelvis.

Cara's eyes widened.

Ethan's grip loosened.

She slipped her arms around his neck. Stared into his eyes. And pressed her lips to his.

TEN

This wasn't supposed to be happening. But the soft touch of Cara's lips, the arms clasped around his neck, wiped all coherent thought from Ethan's mind in an instant. And when her lips opened, it was pure instinct and desperate desire that had him responding too, slipping his tongue into her mouth to deepen the kiss.

She moaned.

Desire flashed through Ethan's entire body in a molten wave.

The movement of his legs kept them upright, but the sure and certain knowledge that he was drowning, in way over his head, burned with every kick.

Her hands were in his hair, and she kissed him

with such abandon, such desperation, that he couldn't possibly resist. With his arm clutching her tight, he needed the ground under his feet. "I need to stand," he murmured against her mouth.

Cara eased away. Her eyelids fluttered open. He swam her to the shallows, and put her feet and his firmly back on solid ground.

Her fingers stroked his neck. Blue eyes gazed into his.

"That was crazy." Ethan loosened his grip. "Too much sun, maybe?"

"Maybe," Cara bit her lip. "Maybe not. Maybe it happened for a reason."

He touched the clasp of her bikini top beneath his fingers, and slid his hand down to the dip at the bottom of her spine. "You know I'm no one's idea of a long term prospect." He needed to warn her off, needed to douse the light in her eyes before he took her up on her unspoken offer. Kissed her like every molecule of his being urged him to do.

"Yes, I know that." Her mouth curved. "But I'm not looking for long-term. I'm not looking for *ever*. But being in your arms..." Warm pink colored her pale cheeks. "It felt right." Her gaze pinned him, daring him to refute her words, to tell her he hadn't felt the same.

"It's normal that you'd feel different, now you're out of Ireland."

She shook her head.

"You've lost everything."

She nodded.

"You're off kilter."

"Maybe."

That word again. He couldn't look away, couldn't step back and add air between their bodies, or hide his reaction to her nearness.

Cara touched his jaw, stroked a finger over his ear. "Or maybe I just want you."

Ethan's heart thundered. "Dammit, Cara, I'm only human." He stepped away from her then, fighting to resist her lips' lure, which was darned difficult with his arms around her. "Don't play with me. Don't tell me you want something from me that you really shouldn't."

Cara wrapped her arm around her torso. "Why shouldn't I want you? I'm human, aren't I?"

Anger welled up in Ethan. She didn't want him; she wanted bloody Crash Carrigan. Just like all the women he'd met in America, she wanted the love 'em and leave 'em cardboard cutout he played on screen. He rubbed a hand through his hair. "I'm not him."

"Not who?" Cara stepped closer.

"I'm Ethan, remember? Your old friend, Ethan. Reliable, non-sexy Ethan." *Not a Hollywood invention,* he longed to add, but couldn't bear to see her reaction. She would never want to hurt him. Would never, or at least, had never come on to him before. And if she wasn't so confused by recent events, this wouldn't be happening, would it?

"I know who you are." Her eyes blazed with truth. "You're my old friend, Ethan. Reliable, honest and true. You'd never hurt me." Her gaze skittered away to the azure water. "You're right. I've never seen you as sexy before, but right now..." her gaze fixed his again, with desire deep in their depths. "I'm finding you very sexy. I'm sorry if that makes you feel uncomfortable, but I'm not going to lie to you." She swirled her arms in the water. Then took a step toward the beach.

Ethan's hand immediately clutched her arm. "Wait."

She stilled.

"Do you know what you're doing? Do you know what you want?"

Cara's lips parted. "I know what I want. But it looks like I'm not going to get it. I'm sorry." She turned away.

Ethan stepped up, pulled her back close against his still aroused body. "You know I want you. I can't hide it, and I'm damned if I'll be sorry for it." He ran his thumb over her bottom lip. "I've never felt desire for you before...before I saw you in that ridiculous Winnie The Pooh costume. Since then..." Ethan grimaced. He couldn't find the words to tell her, and she'd think he was crazy. Having lustful thoughts about his best friend when her life was in crisis was just plain wrong. He dropped her arm.

"Since the fair?" Cara whispered. "You felt it too?"

"Every soft, silky inch," Ethan's voice matched hers. "Holding you was torture."

Cara's slow smile showcased her dimples. "For me too, I thought I was going mad," she admitted. She rested her palms against his chest. "So, let's get this right. You're attracted to me." She glanced down his body. "I'm burning up for you. You don't do long-term, and I don't want it either. We're here, alone in your house for the next couple of weeks, we've been friends forever, and neither of us will hurt the other."

Ethan felt his head jerk up and down in unspoken agreement.

"Please. Kiss me."

CARA'S LIPS TINGLED. The sound of blood rushing in her head was echoed by the soft kiss of the waves against shore. The crease between Ethan's dark brows flattened out. His incredible eyes, surrounded by damp lashes, seemed to shift in chocolate color from milk to dark.

His hand stroked over her hair, tilted up her chin. "No regrets?"

"No regrets."

Slowly, deliberately, he covered her mouth with his own. And her heart almost burst. His mouth was delicious. Addictive. She craved him like she craved Rocky Road, unashamedly. The sand was firm against her soles, but inside it felt as though the sands of her existence were shifting. When this was over, they'd go back to being friends. He meant too much to her to let the little matter of lovemaking get between them, spoil their friendship.

Cool water splashed against her breasts, tightening her nipples into bullets.

Ethan flipped her somehow, unfastened bikini top into the water, cupped her face in both hands, and continued kissing her.

She snuggled close, feeling his light dusting of chest hair against her naked breasts.

His mouth burned a trail down her neck, as his hands cupped her breasts. As his thumbs rubbed her nipples she gasped, and let her head tilt up to the sun. She had known she wanted him, but had no idea how much. How much it was possible to want to make love to another human being.

His fingers hooked into her bikini briefs, stroking her, and toying with the strings at her hip.

Cara trailed a hand down his chest and pressed her pelvis against his. With a growl, Ethan pulled back. "Inside, now."

She glanced at the shore, at the large, bare expanse of silver sand. In the water, she at least had the chance of dipping below the waves if a stranger passed by. But topless on the beach...

Her hands slipped over her breasts. Ethan smiled. Then searched the water nearby for her bikini top.

"Here." It hung from his fingertips. "Slip your arms in and turn around."

Cara did as ordered, feeling the quick brush of his fingers at her back as he attached the clasp. The overwhelming passion of their clinch had dissipated in the moments since. Now, embarrassment niggled as she swiveled back to him.

He glanced at her chest, and frowned. "Aw, I miss 'em."

Laughter bubbled up. She let it free, let the wind carry it away. With one sentence, he'd swept away the awkwardness. Surely it would be the same after they slept together?

His teeth flashed white in the sunshine. A warm hand grasped hers as they ran out of the water together.

Barefoot, Cara climbed the steps to the beach house, the heat of Ethan's palms at her waist sending shivers of excitement through her. In mere moments they were inside his large bedroom. The door closed, and he backed her up against it, then claimed her lips again.

Now, at last, with no water to shield him, she gazed at his chest, his washboard stomach, the board shorts that hung low on his hips. And let her fingers follow the path her eyes had. His skin was hot beneath her fingers.

"You're killing me," Ethan moaned, kissing across her cheekbones, and then claiming her mouth again.

Blood roared in Cara's ears as his tongue tangled with hers. He must have unfastened her bikini again, for his hands cupped her naked breasts.

"You're beautiful," he murmured against her clavicle, then claimed one tip with his warm mouth.

The tug of his lips sparked an answering ache in her core. Cara gasped, and reached a hand into the waistband of his board shorts. With a muttered oath, Ethan moved, and stripped them off.

Her hand curled around his length, as he undid the ties at the side of her bikini bottoms, and pushed them to the polished wooden floor.

Desperation pounded through her as fast as her

heartbeat. To have him, all of him, inside her. He cupped her, and her leg lifted to bring her closer, thigh sliding against thigh.

"We need a condom. Hang on." Ethan lifted her against his body, and her legs wrapped around his hips. His hands gripped her bottom, keeping her in place as he strode to the bed and laid her carefully upon it. He pulled open a drawer on the bedside table, withdrew a small foil packet and quickly sheathed himself. Then ran his hands over her stomach and over her hipbones. "You're so white—so perfect."

You're perfect too. The thought tumbled through Cara's mind, but remained unspoken as his head lowered to the juncture of her thighs.

She couldn't speak, couldn't think of anything but Ethan, and what he was doing to her. How had she thought she'd made love before? The feelings welling up inside her were so powerful, so abandoned, she couldn't help but raise her hips and clamp her eyes tight shut as her hands tangled in his hair.

"Ethan." The word escaped as a throaty moan.

Ethan's hand moved to replace his mouth, and he quickly kissed his way up her body to her mouth. "I'm here," he murmured, as his length nudged against her.

She wanted him, needed him inside. Her eyes

opened, staring into his. She held her breath as, deliciously slowly, he entered her.

His face changed, and his lashes fluttered closed as their bodies started to move, first slowly as she adjusted to his length, then faster and faster.

Cara's heart pounded. She couldn't seem to get enough air, and heard her own breathing accelerate, reaching, ever reaching for the crescendo. She couldn't hold back the sounds tumbling from her mouth, couldn't hold back...

In a fevered wave, they crested the wave together, and plunged, in freefall, over the other side.

IN PASSION'S AFTERMATH, Ethan curled around Cara, one palm flat against her hip, while the other curled around her torso, holding her close.

She'd been so passionate, so desperate for him, that her excitement had fed his own, and brought him to the most powerful climax of his entire life. And when the sex was over, the lovemaking continued.

They'd tumbled together, unable to stop touching. Her hands on his face, her soft, swollen mouth, her tiny smile as she gazed into his eyes, all tied him closer with silken threads. Made him want to be in her arms forever.

He breathed in the ocean scent of her hair. Kissed her ear. "I need a shower," he whispered. "Wash the salt off."

"Mmm, sounds good." She shifted in his arms, as his hand cupped one bare breast. "I'll join you."

The huge shower had been built for two, with multiple jets that soaked the occupants from different directions. Ethan stood under the water and reached for the shampoo.

She angled her head under a jet, soaking her hair, and he poured shampoo into his palm, angled her close and gently soaped her hair. Her chin tilted up. Her eyes were closed, and he paid careful attention to make sure none of the lather went into her eyes.

With her eyes closed she couldn't judge him. Couldn't see that his feelings must be written all over his face in the sappiest expression known to man. His fingers massaged behind her ears, fingers sliding in the slippery foam. She meant so much to him, was so precious. His thumb swept across her temples, pushing the soapy hair back. He was obsessing over the beauty of her cheekbones, admiring her freckles, and thinking she was the most beautiful girl in the world.

Ethan shook water drops off his hair, and eased away. "You can rinse now."

He poured shampoo into his own palm and rubbed it roughly over his head. He'd agreed to a casual fling. Had told himself making love with Cara wouldn't change anything between them. But somewhere, somehow, everything had changed.

ELEVEN

They were dancing, naked. On a white sandy beach by moonlight.

The firm press of a mouth against her lips. Cara's eyes cracked open.

Ethan stood by the side of the bed, fully dressed in a pair of worn jeans and a black shirt. "I have to go to work. The car's here," he murmured.

Cara's eyes flicked to the alarm clock on the bedside table. Five o'clock. *Five a.m.?* Where had the night gone? She started to sit up, but Ethan's hand on her shoulder eased her back to the pillow. "Stay where you are. It's early, and you need your sleep." He smiled. "We didn't get much last night, and you must be jetlagged."

Cara's face heated. Once they'd climbed back into bed, she couldn't resist wrapping around him again, with predictable results. Another couple of times during the night their bodies had found each other in the darkness. After all that, she should feel sated. Instead, she felt like pulling him right back into bed with her again. It was going to be a tiring few weeks.

"I won't be back until late. We're doing an evening shoot tonight." He stepped away from the bed, and gestured to a set of keys on the bedside table. "You can take it easy, or go shopping. Take the Aston." He grinned. "But don't wreck it."

"Would I?" *Hopefully, he wouldn't remember.*

"You should be okay as long as you don't try to squeeze into any tight parking spaces."

He remembered. She'd never live down the fact that her early forays into driving had included a memorable event where she'd tried to park in the supermarket car-park, and scraped the side of one car on the way in, and another, on the way out.

"I'll be careful."

"Call if you need anything. There's food in the fridge. I won't be back until after midnight." He hovered by the doorway, as if reluctant to leave.

"Okay." She wanted to hug him goodbye, but didn't have the bravery to climb out of bed naked in front of him—not now, in the cold light of day. She pulled the duvet up to her ears. "I might not get out of bed all day."

Ethan's mouth twitched. "I know you—you'll be on the beach straight after breakfast." He glanced at the bedside clock. "Better go." But still he stayed, watching her with a strange expression in his eyes.

"Take care," Cara said.

Ethan's lips pursed. "You too." Then he turned and moments later, the front door slam signaled that he'd gone.

Silence buzzed in her ears. She reached for Ethan's pillow, wrapped her arms around it, and breathed in his familiar scent. *Oh dear. She was in danger of falling for her best friend.* She propped the pillow on top of her own, and gazed out of the floor-length expanse of glass to the day beyond.

In the pale morning, all traces of the day before had been raked from the sand by nature. Below, the ocean glittered dark blue, like a precious jewel. Wave after wave reached shore, in a ballet as old as time. Waking up here each morning would be heaven.

She sighed and snuggled back under the duvet. In a month, this would all be a memory.

Five-thirty. Way to early to get up, with all day and a solitary night stretching before her. But her mind was racing, and the appeal of bed had vanished the moment she woke to find Ethan out of it.

She wandered into the huge bathroom, and eyed the whirlpool tub. Maybe it was a Jacuzzi? It was an improvement on her old iron tub at home, that was for sure. A small bottle of liquid was on the shelf. The fancy French label defied translation, but she twisted it open and had a sniff. Definitely manly, with top-notes of pine, and mid notes of sandalwood.

Cara turned the faucets, sploshed in a generous amount of the emerald liquid, and went downstairs to make herself a cup of coffee to drink while luxuriating.

Five minutes later, cup in hand, she wandered back into the bathroom.

Acres of stiff white micro-bubbles foamed over the Jacuzzi's lip, like overwhipped egg white.

Cara gasped, and put her coffee on the sink back, cursing as it tipped on the uneven surface and splashed into the sink.

The bubbles had crested the rim, and were sliding to the tiled floor.

She stood there, unsure of exactly which mess to clean up first, legs frozen for a microsecond. Then darted to the Jacuzzi, switched off the faucets, and pressed the lever to release the plug. With shaking arms, she bent and scooped as much of the foam as she could from the floor. She eyed the tub. And puffed out a relieved breath as the level fell, and the foam sank an inch or two.

That disaster under control, she grabbed a couple of fluffy bathsheets from the heated towel-rack, and dropped them atop the mess on the floor.

A drip of coffee, which had splashed over the rim of the sink and slowly slid down the outside of the basin, fell dead centre on a pristine white bathsheet, staining it dark brown.

The day, which had previously stretched out with nothing to fill it, was filling fast. Declogging the Jacuzzi, washing and drying the towels—hopefully Ethan'd have some stain remover...

Her cell phone rang in the other room.

Cara rubbed her arms down Ethan's robe, smearing it with foam. Then gave up, and pulled off the entire thing and chucked it in the corner, before dashing to the door. She had to get there before it stopped ringing...

It stopped.

And she was standing by the full-length window, in the nude.

Cara snatched her clothes from the floor and dragged them on. Ethan had promised the beach was private, and that no one would be able to sneak a photograph of them, but you couldn't be too careful.

She scrolled through her phone calls to see whose call she'd missed. *Private.* Hmm. The phone vibrated, and then rang again. Cara answered it.

"Cara?" The voice was unfamiliar, with an American accent. Who could be calling her? Maybe it was Ethan's assistant, Maggie.

"Yes," Cara said. "Who's this?"

A hesitation. Then the caller spoke. "Cara, you may not have seen it yet, but I wanted to know if you have any comment on the story on the cover of today's National Inquisitor? Let me read you the headline, *Ethan Quinn stole my girl.* It continues, *heartbroken Michael Maguire...*"

Cara's legs wobbled. She eased down onto the bed, clutching the cell to her ear. "Who is this?"

"This is the National Inquisitor, ma'am." The female voice continued, "Do you have a comment?"

Cara bit her tongue. She had plenty. The lying weasel, the rotten swine...She pulled in a deep breath. "I haven't seen the story, so at this point I have no comment," she replied, glad her voice was calm and even. A thought struck her. "How did you get this number?"

"Mr. Maguire gave us this number, ma'am."

A blood red haze clouded Cara's vision. "Goodbye," she forced out through gritted teeth.

She terminated the call, threw the cell on the bed, and gave in to the overwhelming need to let loose all the pent up curses she'd been carefully holding back.

ETHAN'S FEET were covered in bloody cuts.

He walked into the makeup trailer, sat, and propped them up on the stool before the makeup artist. "Isn't there a quick way to get them off?"

Doris smiled as continuity photographed his feet with a Polaroid in case of reshoots. "You know better than that, Ethan."

It had taken two hours to painstakingly create his wounds, and would take half that to remove them. A long rip on his jeans' thigh revealed a large knife slash, built up with silicone carefully molded and filled with scar and fresh fake blood.

"Want something to read?" Doris waved at the newspapers on the desk. "I've got most of them."

"I bet you haven't got the Inquisitor," said Maggie from the doorway of the trailer. She clutched a tabloid in her hands.

"No, I don't think I have." Doris picked up her

palette knife and starting to peel off the scars on Ethan's feet. "I don't like that one, it's a rag."

"I never miss it." Maggie's mouth tightened. "Although I wish I had this morning."

"Are you going to tell me why?" Ethan asked, forcing patience into his voice. There was obviously some problem Maggie thought he needed to know; he wished she'd just get on with it. "Because I could really do with a coffee."

Maggie slumped down on a chair. "I'll get you one in a minute. I need to show you this first." She flattened the tabloid on her knee, and smoothed out the cover with the flat of her palm. "I'm warning you, you're not going to like it."

Ethan reached for the paper. Underneath the libelous headline, a photograph of Michael Maguire stared out with what anyone who had eyes could plainly tell was a faked-up devastated expression. "The creep," he muttered. "What's he getting out of this?"

"Problem, dear?" Doris asked.

"Payback?" Maggie suggested.

Ethan threw the tabloid to the floor. "Cara's ex-boyfriend." He glanced at the storyline, "Not ex-fiancé as they say here, cheated on her. She's my friend. And she's lost her job as a result of some ridiculous pictures taken last week."

"Money then," Maggie said helpfully. "I suppose someone paid him for his story."

"Well, you know what they say you should do if the press tell lies about you, dear. Don't you? I've had all of them here at my table, one time or another. With the most filthy lies and intrusions into their private lives. The only thing to do is to take the high ground. If you get into a war of words with the press, you'll never win." Doris piled a sliver of bloodied silicone onto the growing pile on the table. They looked like gutted anchovies.

"It makes you seem really irresistible, as though Cara couldn't help herself," Maggie muttered. "I guess that can't be bad for your reputation."

"For what, my reputation as a lady-killer who has so little respect for people that he seduces a bride-to-be?" Anger bit in Ethan's stomach. "That's not who I am, and I'll be damned if I'll let it go." He glanced at Maggie. "I need to talk to my publicist, and my lawyer. And..."

"I'll get you some coffee first," Maggie finished.

Ethan jerked his head in a curt nod. "And grab me a laptop." While his body was occupied, he could at least check the web, see how bad it was.

The older lady wiped the fresh fake blood from the left side of his foot. "How's your friend bearing up? This must be terrible for her."

"She doesn't deserve this. I brought her out to

Malibu to shield her, but that doesn't seem to have worked out, does it?"

"It must be worse in Ireland, if he's saying these things." Doris picked up the spatula again, and worked at a scar on the top of his foot. "At least she can talk to you about it."

She was alone in the beach house. Doubtless lying out on the sand, soaking up the sun's rays and relaxing. The last thing she needed was to know about the poison being peddled with her name attached to it. There'd be plenty of time to shatter her good mood. And with any luck, he'd be able to get his publicist, Melissa Brown, out to brainstorm a response tomorrow morning. Filming wasn't starting until the afternoon.

He leaned back in the chair and closed his eyes. His mind drifted back to earlier that morning. He'd untangled her long languid limbs from around him and regretfully climbed out of bed before dawn broke. When the car had arrived to take him on set, and she'd woken, he'd felt the tug to her again, the moment her unfocussed gaze collided with his. He hadn't wanted to leave. And he always wanted to leave. No matter how good the night before had been, he was always keen to get back to work, to disengage himself from any lingering emotions.

With Cara, it was different. He wanted to spend the day with her. Wanted to show her around the area, and spend long hours over dinner in his favorite restaurant, listening to her laugh. Heck, he'd be happy to just rub sun-cream over that milk-white skin, and fetch her drinks all day.

Warm water splashed over his toes, bringing him back to reality with a jerk.

"That's one." Doris shifted her stool around, and started on his other foot.

TWELVE

Whenever she was worried, Cara would pick up the phone to Ethan. But, for the first time ever, she couldn't do that. He was working. Busy. So busy, it would be wrong to bother him. The fact that Michael had chosen to blacken Ethan's name filled her with guilt. He didn't deserve it. Had done nothing, apart from be a true friend when she'd needed one.

Telling him could wait. But clearing up the mess she'd made of his home couldn't.

It took copious rinsing to banish the suds from the bathtub. By the time the towels were washed and in the drier, hunger was biting chunks out of her stomach, so she made a bacon sandwich and carried it over to the laptop on the polished wooden desk in the corner.

She checked her email. One message, from Suz. Her gut clenched as she read through her friend's diatribe about Michael's behavior, apparently he'd been telling all and sundry that Cara had 'run-off' with Ethan. If Suz was incensed now, just wait till she caught a glimpse of The National Inquisitor.

She tapped the tabloid's title into the search engine, and sucked in a deep breath as she found the link to the online version. She closed her eyes as she clicked the link. This wasn't going to be pretty, but she needed to know exactly what he'd said, in order to report to Ethan later.

She read through the article with disgust and growing dismay. Not only had Michael trashed her reputation, but he'd also been photographed looking distraught on the front cover. There was mention of Carethan, apparently a mash up of her and Ethan's names. The photographs that had flooded the Irish papers were reproduced too, and a little note at the end of the article asked for people with any photographs to send them in to the paper.

With a groan, she remembered the girls at the airport. Would they succumb to the lure of payment and send in the pictures of her and Ethan they'd smiled for, the day before?

She flicked to the two-page virtual spread titled

'Women He's Loved and Left.' Many small pictures filled the screen. Ethan, with his arm around a Brazilian model in one, kissing an actress in another. Holding hands with Aoife Fitzpatrick in a third. Cara rubbed her hand over her eyes. Dancing with a statuesque blonde, having dinner with a redhead. And, if the copy was to be believed, he'd seduced and abandoned all of them.

She stared at the picture of Aoife. At least she knew the truth about this relationship—so why was the newspaper reporting Ethan had left Aoife, when the complete opposite was true?

She typed their names into Google, and watched the links appear.

After fifteen minutes, there was only one conclusion she could come to: that Aoife had spread the story of being abandoned, and later revealed a new boyfriend. Painting Ethan as the bad guy, again. Why he hadn't contradicted Aoife's story perplexed her. And made her wonder how many of the women he'd been pictured with were really even ex-girlfriends.

She flicked her hair away from her face with a weary hand. Dealing with these lies was beyond her. Should she refute the charges leveled against her in the press, or take the high ground and ignore them? Given the fact that she'd actually gone all out to seduce Ethan, was Michael right—had she mentally thrown him over the moment she felt attraction for Ethan as he pulled her from that damned costume?

Pushing back the chair, she went to the bedroom to change into her swimsuit. Yes, she'd been attracted to Ethan, back then. But she hadn't been sure enough of Michael to commit to him, and when she'd heard of his betrayal, she'd been stunned and hurt. Even if Ethan wasn't in the picture, she would have broken off all contact with him. And he hadn't even stuck around to hear her reaction, had just run away as fast as his legs could carry him.

In the article, he revealed that he was working for a large American company based in Dublin. Which meant his foray from Donabridge had been successful. She knew her father, he wouldn't be able to fire Michael for being a snake, but he could have made working for him hell, and wouldn't have hesitated to make his annoyance and displeasure clear. Michael had managed to get another job before that happened.

Throwing mud at Cara would cleverly mitigate against any possibility that Cara's father might give him a rotten reference.

She pulled a clean towel from the cupboard, stuck her feet into her thongs, and stepped out into the warm, Malibu sunlight. Bloody Michael had done enough damage for one day. She was determined not to obsess about him any longer.

THEY WERE due to finish shooting at eleven. Finding out about the latest intrusion into his private life had focused Ethan's intent. Given his acting an edge of perfection that ensured he took less takes than normal, and by nine, his entire day's shooting was in the can.

"We don't need you any more tonight," John said. "So if you want to go..." His head tilted, and he squeezed Ethan's arm. "I know you must want to get back."

They hadn't spoken about the press's intrusion, but everyone on set must have seen the tabloid by now. And John was no stranger to paparazzi; he'd know the strain Ethan was under.

"Great. I'll see you tomorrow afternoon, then."

John nodded, and exited the trailer.

By ten, he was waving off the car, and standing on the front doorstep with the paper clutched in his hand. Lights blazed inside; it was too early for Cara to have retired to bed. He'd have to tell her.

The door swung open.

"I thought I heard a car." Cara was dressed in a long loose red dress, her hair glinting with highlights a day in the sun had intensified. Her nose looked pink, and her feet were bare. "You're early."

"I got through it earlier than anticipated." Ethan stepped in, and brushed his lips against hers.

"Keen to get home?" she murmured against his lips.

His hand brushed against the side of her face. "Yes."

Time stood still. If only he didn't have to tell her. Didn't have to snap the thread of attraction tightening between them. He puffed out a frustrated breath.

Cara's gaze flickered to the tabloid he gripped in his other hand. "You've seen it, then?"

"You know about it?" She must have gone out, seen it on the news-stands. Any crazy could have recognized her from the pictures in it. Could have approached her. Ethan's heart dived. He should have phoned, should have warned...

"They phoned my cell this morning. I checked it out online." Cara stepped back, and took the paper from his hand.

Blood roared in Ethan's ears. "They phoned you? How the hell—"

"Michael was kind enough to give them the number," Cara said calmly. "What are we going to do about it?"

She could be calm and collected about it, but

Ethan wanted to punch a hole in the wall. He stalked into the room, heading straight for the whiskey bottle he kept for emergencies in the top cupboard. He splashed a generous amount into two glasses, handed one to Cara, and swallowed a mouthful. The whiskey seared his throat. Its aroma filled his mouth and nostrils. It didn't take the edge off.

"That lying—"

"—snake? Turd? Asshole? I'm surprised the air in here isn't blue, I've cursed him so much." She smiled a tight smile. "After trying them all out, I settled on 'pathetic loser.'" She walked into his arms, and hugged him tight. "I'm sorry. You don't deserve this." Her words were muffled against his chest.

Ethan's heart swelled. She *was worried about him?*

He tilted her chin up, and gazed into her eyes. "I'm well used to it. I'm angry for you."

"They had a field day, pulling out all your previous...they even mentioned Aoife." Her eyes narrowed. "And they got that totally wrong. Why does the world think you dumped her, Ethan? You told me all about it; I can't believe you took the rap for the breakup."

"They get everything wrong, that's the way the press are." Ethan rubbed his hand over his hair.

"The moment I arrived in America, they tagged me with the Irish bad-boy thing. Half the women they photographed me with I've never slept with." He opened the paper that she'd tossed on the table, and stabbed at the pictures with a finger. "This was a first date, after which I dropped her home. Her career needed a boost, so her publicist invented a story. And this one." He felt his lip curl as he pointed to another picture. "This is a still from a movie, for Christ's sake. I never so much as went out for a drink with her."

He slipped an arm around her and held her tight. "I'm no angel," he murmured against her hair. "But I'm no devil either. It suits the image they've built to paint me as one."

"And Aoife?" she questioned, not letting him off the hook for a moment.

"Aoife..." It all seemed so long ago. He guessed he must have thought he was in love with her; it had certainly hurt enough at the time. But the fact that she'd given an interview to a woman's magazine, saying sadly that things just hadn't worked out between them, had been all that the press needed to run with the 'wounded Irish beauty' angle. She'd done well with the publicity in the years since. Her interior design business was thriving, and she'd even had the cheek to send him an invite to her wedding next month.

He'd taken a perverse pleasure in burning it in the fireplace. They'd sold the pictures for the wedding to a glossy magazine, and doubtless his non-attendance would lose them a couple of hundred thousand from the fee, but he'd be damned it he'd play the ex for the cameras. "At the time, I didn't care enough to put the story straight."

Cara's eyes sparked fire. She pulled away, and put her hands on her hips. "Well, it's about time they stopped putting these lies out there." She tossed her hair back. "They need to divorce the man from the role." Her mouth tightened. "I've a good mind to phone them up and..."

She looked so fierce, so protective, he couldn't hold back a smile. "Going into the ring for me, Cara?"

"Damn right. And I'm aiming for a knock-out."

She'd do it too, the truth blazed from her eyes, and extinguished the anger that had blazed thorough him like a forest fire all day. He reached for her shoulders, felt the tension in them, and kneaded gently. The words *I love you,* ran through his head. A week ago, he'd be able to say it, but now they'd slept together saying it felt too serious, too forever.

He'd once told another woman he loved her. There was no way he was putting himself on the line for heartache again. But nothing else seemed to fit. He lowered his head and kissed her. Letting his lips tell her what his voice couldn't.

"My publicist will be here tomorrow morning. We'll work out a plan of attack then."

Her fingers crept under the hem of his T-shirt. Soft fingers stroked his belly. "Let's go to bed," she whispered.

WHILE ETHAN SHOWERED, Cara dressed in her sexy, grey silk nightie and slipped between the cool cotton sheets. After the panic of the morning, she'd swam in the ocean and picked shells off the shore for hours, letting the beauty of the day wash over her like the water that rushed over her toes at the water's edge. Taking her irritations with it, as it receded.

She was stealing time in paradise. In a few scant weeks, she'd be back to reality, and would fight her battles then. The conversation with Ethan had reignited her indignation. Especially when he'd confirmed her suspicions about the women he'd been accused of hurting. Ethan wasn't a forever type of guy, there was no use pretending he was. The experience with Aoife had left him wary and unable to commit. But he wasn't a bad guy either, and the fact that the press had decided to label him one burned.

Ethan walked out of the bathroom with a towel slung low on his hips.

Cara's mouth dried. All thought vanished in an instant at the look in his eyes.

He walked to the bed. "I like your nightie," he murmured as he pulled back the sheet, whisked off the towel and pulled her close. "Does it feel as silky as it looks?" His hands smoothed over the silk, warming the flimsy fabric and the skin beneath. "Mmm, it does."

And as his mouth teased her nipple through the silk, Cara ran her hands through his hair, and surrendered to sensation.

THIRTEEN

When Melissa Brown arrived at the beach house the next morning, Cara liked her instantly. Her silver cap of hair was expertly cut, and her muted makeup emphasized her patrician features. She was wearing an unstructured, black skirt and tunic combo, which must have come from a top designer, so elegant was its simplicity.

She walked into the sitting room, four inch heels clicking on the wooden floor, and placed her briefcase on the coffee table. "Right, let's get to it," she said eyeing Ethan. She glanced at Cara. "I need to find out how much of this is true and how much is a complete fabrication. And we need to decide what, if anything, we're going to do about it."

Ethan sat with Cara on the sofa opposite

Melissa. He covered her hand with his own. "They can say what they like about me, but I'm not happy that they're making Cara the focus. She's not a public figure."

Melissa's eyebrow arched. "Maybe not a week ago, but now..." She cleared her throat. "I'm afraid all that has changed." Her voice lowered with sympathy evident in her deep tones. "The photographs in the Irish paper," she flicked open her briefcase and pulled out the photograph of Cara half-naked in Ethan's arms, "this one in particular, ignited interest in Cara—who she is, what she means to you." She shrugged. "There's no way of putting that particular genie back in the bottle."

Ethan's mouth set in a thin line. "I've already lost Cara her job. And any prospect of getting another as a teacher in Ireland, because of it."

Cara pulled her hand from under his. "Hang on a second, Ethan. You're not to blame for this." Her eyes couldn't stray away from the picture, which lay on the table. She reached for it, and examined it. "The reason this picture lost me my job was because I was barely clothed in it. That was my fault. I never should have climbed into the costume in my underwear."

Since her teens, she'd been concerned about preserving her reputation, not getting into trouble, and making sure she'd never see disappointment in her parents' faces again. But being here with Ethan, seeing the liberties the press took with the truth, had opened her eyes to the way that life really was. Through no fault of her own, her reputation was shredded. And, what was today's news would be tomorrow's waste paper. Ethan couldn't feel responsible for the words written by any journalist.

Melissa laced her fingers together, showcasing vivid red fingernails that curved like talons, presumably for ripping the press apart. "I agree. The picture would have considerably less impact if you were clothed. But combined with the photographs of you both at the fundraiser in Ireland, looking so happy," she took another couple of pictures from the briefcase and slid them across the table, "people saw what they wanted to see. A couple entranced with each other."

Ethan lifted one picture, and Cara picked up another. In both, they were smiling into the camera, obviously at ease.

"Carethan was born," Melissa murmured.

Ethan glanced up. "And the fact that we weren't—" he swallowed—"involved, doesn't that count for anything?"

"Not really," Melissa said. "These pictures hint at an intimacy, a closeness between you, that captured the public imagination. Rather like all of the great love stories in history, people want to believe that if you're not already in love, you will be soon." She pulled out a sheaf of paper. "These are printouts from the Carethan hashtag, and the majority of tweets are about what a great couple you make. How it looks as though Ethan cares, and about how much the tweeps want you to get together."

"Christ." Ethan ran a hand through his hair.

Cara's heart dipped. Would it be such a bad thing to be *involved* with her?

"Moving on." Melissa opened a copy of the National Inquisitor. "This is another matter. In this article, Michael makes concrete claims about Cara breaking off her engagement and leaving him. And names you as the guilty party." She stared at Ethan. "If this isn't true, we can sue him, although it will be difficult to win without proof. The danger is that it will keep the entire affair in the public domain for much longer."

"They paint Ethan unfairly as a womanizer. Michael and I were never engaged. He'd proposed, but I hadn't accepted. Ethan hit him when he saw Michael cheating on me," Cara said. "Ethan behaved honorably. It's awful that Michael should—"

"Lie?" Melissa asked. "It wouldn't be the first time someone has lied about Ethan. And it won't be the last. Unfortunately that's the business he's in."

She tapped her front teeth with a fingernail and stared out the window for long moments. “People want to see you together. If you’re just friends, or have other lovers, then I think you need to set the record straight. I know the studio is keen to give the impression that you and Dee have a flirtation going on, Ethan. As pre-publicity for the next movie.”

Ethan shook his head. “I’m not agreeing to that. Not for a minute. I’m sure Dee won’t want to either, we can’t stand each other.”

Melissa’s eyebrows rose in two perfect arcs. “That bad?”

“That bad,” Ethan confirmed. “The truth is...” He paused for a significant moment. “Cara and I have grown closer since this whole mess. But that’s no one’s business but our own.”

Cara reached for his hand and squeezed it.

“With the firestorm of interest in your relationship at the moment, I doubt you can afford the luxury of ignoring the press right now,” Melissa said. “Did you know the paparazzi are camped outside the gates?”

Ethan cursed. “Many?”

“A couple of dozen. They surrounded the car and were taking pictures of me when I came in. A couple even shot pictures through the gates when they opened. I saw them in my rear-view mirror.” She shoved the pictures and papers back into her briefcase. "The best thing to do is give the public what they want. Which is, pictures of both of you together. Be open about your relationship. Refuting the minutae of how you got together might come across as an attempt to blacken Michael's name. He's sold his story, and any public fight will just give him the opportunity to sell updates. If you deal with the situation as it is now," she leaned forward, resting her elbows on her knees, "then Michael's story will quickly become yesterday's news."

"I don't want Cara followed everywhere. I can't be with her all the time, filming is still ongoing, and I want her to be safe."

Melissa nodded. "Of course. She might be photographed, but she's unlikely to come to any harm. It's inconvenient, sure, but..."

"I'll be fine," Cara said.

"My advice would be to take the high road, and not to panic," Melissa soothed. "What's done is done, and the best way to move forward is to appear together at a couple of functions, to pose nicely for photographs. That should diffuse the frenzy that's building up. People will soon lose interest and focus on the next hint of scandal. You could even tweet something innocuous to calm the twitter stream."

Ethan puffed out a breath. "I hate having to play these games." He crossed his arms over his chest. "And I hate twitter."

"Don't I know it!" Melissa laughed. "Getting you to tweet is like pulling teeth." Her eyes softened. "But I really think it would be worth it, Ethan."

Ethan stared into Cara's eyes. "What do you think?" he asked, caring evident in the depths of his eyes. "Are you ready to face the press?"

Cara glanced down at her jeans and bare feet. "Maybe I should change first."

Ethan stood. "Okay, I'll tweet that we thank my followers for their concern, and are happy together. Will that do it?"

Melissa nodded.

"I'll make some coffee while you get ready," Ethan said. "Then we'll walk to the gate and give them a photo-op."

HE WANTED to hold her hand.

But Cara crossed her arms and kicked the ground with one sneaker-clad toe as the gate swung open.

The whirring cameras sounded as though a swarm of cicadas had landed outside the gates. There were at least ten, maybe fifteen photographers jostling for position, and as they caught sight of Ethan, the air filled with shouted questions.

Ethan stepped forward and held out his arms. He forced a smile. "I have a quick statement, and then I'll take questions." The photographers kept taking photographs, but at least stopped shouting.

"Cara and I know you're keen to get pictures, and ask questions." Despite what he'd agreed with Melissa, Ethan couldn't let the impression stand that Cara was a casual lay he'd picked up on his last visit to Ireland. "Cara and I are old friends. A lot of inaccurate information has been in the press over the last couple of days. When I was in Ireland recently, Cara was recovering from a relationship that had already ended." He drew out the last bit, emphasizing the truth of the matter. "I asked her to come and stay with me in Malibu for a short holiday."

A shout from a rather sweaty journalist at the back, "Are you sleeping together?"

Ethan swallowed back his anger, and fixed the journalist with a stare. "My relationship with Cara is our business." He clenched his teeth. "However, I'm aware there is great interest in it, so I will say that we are in a relationship, yes."

He stepped closer to Cara, and reached for her hand.

"Questions?"

Shouts came quick and fast. “Cara, how do you feel about your fiancé’s article?” “Cara, how long are you staying?” “Ethan, are you talking marriage?”

He wanted to stand in front of her. To shove her back behind the safety of the gate, away from prying eyes.

She squeezed his hand. “I’ll answer some of those,” she said in a voice so quiet the paparazzi fell quiet to listen. “I was never engaged, and the end of my relationship had nothing to do with Ethan,” she said in a calm voice. “I’m staying for a couple of weeks. I’ve never been to America before, and Malibu is fabulous. I’m looking forward to seeing a lot more of your beautiful country while I’m here.”

The cynical faces softened the moment they caught her smile.

“I think I can answer the last question that was aimed at Ethan.”

He held his breath.

“Ethan and I aren’t thinking marriage.”

“We’re happy to pose for photographs for a few minutes, but we have to leave in half an hour.” He snaked an arm around Cara’s shoulders.

“Kiss her!” someone shouted.

Ethan felt a smile tug at his lips. “I don’t think so, guys. Sorry.”

“What about the pic in your underwear, Cara? Any comment?”

Before she could respond, Ethan cut in. "We really don't have any further comment about that."

Cara nodded.

They posed for photographs for five minutes, then Ethan stepped away from Cara's side. "That's it." He softened his words with a smile. "Thanks very much."

Cameras lowered. "Thanks for coming out, Ethan," a tall thin man at the front said. "Appreciate it."

Ethan pressed a button, waved briefly as the gates slid closed, and blew out a breath as the paparazzi were shielded from view. With luck they would leave. But his stomach clenched with nerves at the thought that they may not. And an overzealous person might even find a way over the wall and pester Cara while he wasn't there. Might photograph her on the beach. She needed his protection, even if she didn't want it.

He glanced at his watch. "We better get ready—the car will be here soon to take me on set. I want you to come with me."

Cara's eyes lit. "Really?"

"Really. It's about time you saw what I do for a living."

FOUR HOURS LATER, the excitement of being on a movie set was fading. Ethan had introduced her to it seemed like hundreds of people, all of whom had been very welcoming, but curious, and Cara was beginning to feel as though she was in a fishbowl, swimming in ever decreasing circles.

She'd sat in Ethan's chair, and watched him act. Chatted to the makeup department, and even popped in to the costume trailer and had a look at the props. Now, rather than return to watch Ethan run through yet another scene, she sneaked back to the trailer, grabbing a cup of tea on the way.

She sank down into a comfortable armchair, and tucked her feet under her. Cara rooted in her voluminous bag, and pulled out the paperback Juliet had shoved into her hands on the flight over. *Edge of Night.* The cover didn't look as though it was her usual type of reading material, but hadn't Juliet told her not to judge a book by its cover? She opened it, and by the time she'd read the first chapter, she was totally hooked. Juliet's writing was so good she could see why the movie option had been picked up. The main character was complex, finely drawn, and compelling. With an edge of danger and menace that sent shivers up Cara's spine. Any actor would kill for the role.

Cara's legs tingled. She stretched out her legs and rubbed them, turning a page as she did so.

The trailer door creaked open.

"Hi, Cara," Maggie said, looking around. "Is he here?"

"Um..." Cara reluctantly pulled her attention away from *Edge of Night*. "No, I think he's still filming."

"Filming's finished for the day."

Cara glanced at her watch, surprised to see that a couple of hours had passed without her noticing.

"I'll just wait here for him." Maggie closed the door behind her and sat on the loveseat in the corner. "I have to pass on some messages. His agent was trying to get hold of him."

The door pushed open again.

"Hi," Ethan grinned. "Sorry, I got distracted."

A small, dark haired man in a black suit stood behind him. "Cara, this is my agent, Manny Silverstein."

"Ah, you found him then," Maggie interrupted. "I was just coming to tell you, Manny'd been on a few times, Ethan."

Ethan focused his gaze on her. "Are there any other messages I should know about?"

Maggie's head shook from side to side. "That's it."

"Okay."

Maggie's eyebrows rose in silent query.

"I think that's it for today, then, Maggie."

She nodded, and made for the door. "Okay, I'll see you tomorrow."

With a smile, she angled past Manny.

Cara stood, turned down a corner of her book, and shook Manny's extended hand. "Pleased to meet you," she murmured.

Manny's gaze was fixed on the book in her hands. "You're reading *Edge of Night*?" His forehead creased with a frown. "That's weird. I didn't think it was on sale in America yet."

"I met the author on the plane." Cara glanced from Manny to Ethan, wondering why the agent was so perplexed by what she was reading.

"Sit down, Manny." Ethan pointed to the loveseat. "And tell me what's so urgent it'd bring you out of the office."

A sly smile played over Manny lips. He settled on the love seat, and crossed his legs, revealing a flash of sock suspender. "Before I do..." He stared at Cara. "What do you think of the book, any good?"

"It's fantastic," Cara admitted. "The writing is really compelling, and the plot draws you right in."

"And the main character?" Manny glanced at Ethan.

"Really three-dimensional. The sort of character that burrows into your brain, and makes you really wonder what drives him. I haven't read anything so good in a long time." Her school workload had cut into her reading time. She spent the day imparting the classics to a classroom of bored boys, struggling to try and pass on her love of words. At the end of the day she was always exhausted, but never too exhausted to read. Books, and the glimpse they gave into other worlds, were her life.

Manny nodded. "I haven't read it yet. But I've been hearing good things. Brightman Pictures are going to turn it into a movie."

"Brightman?" Cara's head swam. Stephen Brightman was the hottest director in America. Juliet had been modest when she'd said it was going to be made into a movie. With Brightman behind it, it would be a blockbuster.

"Anyway, that's why I said it was weird that you were reading it," Manny continued, beaming at Ethan. "Stephen Brightman rang me this afternoon, and wants you to screen-test for the lead."

FOURTEEN

The discussion with Manny continued through dinner, that they ate with the rest of the crew in the catering double-decker bus, huddled at a table on the upper deck, at the back. Ethan's hand caressed her knee under the table, making it darned difficult to concentrate on the conversation. Luckily, she was there only as an observer, so didn't have to worry too much about it.

When Manny eventually left, they sipped hot coffee from Styrofoam cups.

Cara gazed out at the darkening sky. It would be night by the time they were back in Malibu.

"Penny for them?" Ethan asked, leaning close.

"You've really made a life for yourself here," Cara whispered. Any lingering dreams she been having about Ethan coming home had finally burned up when she'd realized that after this film would be another one. And another. He needed to be here, in America for his career. It was what he'd been working for all his life, from the early days when he went to Dublin stage school.

Donabridge held too many painful memories for him. When his parents' died he'd felt responsible because his father had started drinking again, and he hadn't known it. No matter how she'd tried to tell him his mother had hidden the fact from everyone, Ethan believed he could have made a difference. If he'd been home, he would have known, and could have averted the tragedy.

And her life...

In a few weeks she'd be gone. Back to try to remake some sort of life in Donabridge. Realistically, he couldn't follow. The likelihood of being able to keep a long distance romance going was slim to none. Cara bit her lip, reality sucked.

"Are you regretting last night?" Ethan reached for her hand, and laced his long, tanned fingers through hers. "Because I'm not."

She turned her head to his. Stared into his dark eyes. *Honesty.* Would she tell him the truth, that the thought of their time together trickling away made her heart feel heavy in her chest, or would she lie, and say she was content with what they had, no matter how fleeting?

"I couldn't regret last night." She tried for a smile. "I guess I'm just tired."

This was Ethan's life. Not hers. They'd been flung together by a quirk of fate, tied together by the desires and expectations of a capricious public. And when the time was right, they'd part, and no doubt the press would report that Ethan Quinn had broken another heart.

"There's no more filming for a couple of days. We can sleep late, and then I'll take you to all my favorite places." His lips pressed her temple in a quick kiss.

Cara pulled her hand from his and pushed back her hair. Her past lay in ruins; her future would be lonely without him. But she had now. And, no matter the outcome, she intended to enjoy it.

THE FOLLOWING MORNING, the phone rang over breakfast.

"I thought you should know," Maggie's voice was apologetic. "Zane Blackwell got drunk last night at a strip-club, and took off with a stripper. It's all over the news."

Ethan sighed. Aoife's wedding could be off

then, depending on how things panned out over the next few hours. "Have either of them made a statement?"

"Not yet," Maggie said. "But the stripper is everywhere, telling her story. Apparently they had a wild, sex crazed night, and she has a sex tape to prove it."

Ethan felt nothing. Not even sympathy for the anguish Aoife would doubtless be feeling now her fantasy love life was in tatters. He'd always protected the ones he loved, and he'd loved Aoife, once. But no more. He walked to the security console and flicked on the camera which focused on the area outside the gate. The paparazzi had gone.

One man's scandal was another man's reprieve.

"Thanks for letting me know." Ethan hung up. At least if he were called for a comment, he'd know what the journalist was talking about. It was small minded to rejoice in the freedom the lack of attention gave, but he reveled in it, nonetheless.

"News?" Cara bit into her toast, and poured him another cup of coffee.

"Aoife's fiancé caught in sex tape scandal." He didn't want to dwell on it. Didn't want even the shadow of his ex's distress to fall over their time together.

Cara's smile wobbled. "Was that her?"

"It was Maggie." He swallowed a mouthful of

coffee. "She wanted me to know in case anyone asks for a comment."

"Are you going to call Aoife?" Cara's head tilted to the side. "Because I know..."

"Aoife and I are history. Have been for a long time. Events in her love life aren't anything to do with me, and believe me," he leaned close and wiped a tiny crumb off her top lip, "I'm not even remotely interested in Aoife."

Cara's throat moved. She blinked a couple of times, then lifted her lips to his. "Good," she murmured against his mouth, moments before she kissed him.

The prospect of investigating all that Malibu had to offer alone had never held much appeal, but with Cara by his side, it became fun. In the days that followed, they trekked through Malibu Creek, stopping to watch climbers scaling the Planet of the Apes wall, and continued down the rocky path to Century Lake, with hills of porous lava and striped layers of rock.

They went to Zuma Beach because Cara wanted to check out the Baywatch lifeguards. Shared a pizza in a little restaurant with tables that faced the blue ocean. And talked about everything. When he'd brought Aoife out, she'd always wanted to go to the celebrity haunts, had her head turned by the attention. Cara was the complete opposite.

But of course, she'd always been more interested in spending time with him than being seen, hadn't she?

Not for one moment would Ethan have believed he'd fall for his best friend so quickly, so completely. Their time together was ticking away. He didn't want her to go. Couldn't stand the thought of there being an ocean between them. Laughing with Cara, watching the way the sun glinted in her golden hair, and the way her eyes turned dark navy when he kissed her were becoming so familiar, so needed, that his gut clenched at the thought of being without her.

The matter of her departure lay like a dark boulder between them. He hadn't missed her words to the press that she was staying for a couple of weeks, even when he suggested she should stay longer. Even a month, to see how things panned out between them, was too short. They were going to have to talk about it.

"Wow." Cara looked down at the chocolate dessert the waitress had just delivered to their beachside table. "That's one hell of a pudding."

"If you can't manage it..." Ethan eyed the concoction, regretting choosing only coffee to finish their meal.

Cara waved to the waitress. "Can I have another spoon?"

The blonde grinned, nodded and brought one over.

"I'll share. If you're sure you can risk the calories?" One eyebrow rose. Her gaze scanned his torso.

Ethan surreptitiously tugged up his T-shirt, flashing his abs. "What do you think?"

Cara's tongue swiped over her top lip. She flushed pink. "Stop that," she muttered in a deep voice.

Ethan let his shirt drop, and leaned close, gazing at her lips. "You like?"

Cara shifted on her seat. "You know damn well I like. And if you don't stop looking at me like that..."

"Like what?" Ethan teased, moving his chair closer so he could stroke a hand across her thigh covered in the light cotton of her yellow sundress.

Cara's eyes widened. Her hand landed on top of his, halting his slow exploration of her thigh. "Stop."

"No one's watching."

She picked his hand up, and deposited it on his lap.

"Eat your dessert." She handed him the spoon. Helped herself to a spoonful, and licked the chocolate cream off her lip with barely disguised delight. "Then you can show me how quickly you can drive us home."

ETHAN WAS USELESS AT OBEYING. As she dipped into the dessert again, his jaw line tightened, and he reached for the spoon and put it down on the plate.

"Do you have any idea how sexy you look, eating that bloody cake?" he muttered. "Watching you is torture."

Desire, which was already taking over her entire body, flooded Cara, tightening her nipples beneath the gauzy top of her sundress. Heat pooled between her thighs as his eyes swept over her. Dessert forgotten, she reached for his hand and squeezed it tight. "Let's go."

Her hand rested on his thigh as he drove home as if the hounds of hell were pursuing them. The engine had barely stopped when he jerked her door open, and pulled her out into his arms.

His hands molded her breasts, and with a muttered curse, he picked her up and strode inside, kicking the door shut behind him.

By the sofa, facing the sea, he undid the zip, and pulled the dress down, leaving her standing in only her lacy panties and high heeled sandals. With harsh movements, he quickly stripped, and tumbled her onto the sofa, urgency ripping away finesse as he kissed her frantically, hands cupping her breasts.

Cara's heart raced. Her hands were at the nape of his neck, her fingers brushing his hair, feeling the warmth of his neck. She was shaking. So turned on, she couldn't hold back the moans that escaped her throat.

Ethan pulled down her panties and tossed them over the sofa. His mouth pressed against her neck, lower and lower, each kiss setting off tiny explosions within.

They'd made love all night. And again this morning. But she wanted him with an urgency that defied reason. All that mattered was being closer. Being one. . She reached between their bodies, and stroked him.

Ethan groaned, and she felt him shudder.

"Condom." He eased off her, and reached for his jeans, pulling out a small foil packet and quickly sheathing himself.

As his hand feathered across her hip, Ethan's forehead rested on hers. His dark eyes were almost black as their gazes locked. Time stood still. Cara's heart expanded, beating hard against her ribcage.

"You know I love you, don't you, Cara mia?" He dusted his lips across hers in a soft caress.

Words dried in Cara's throat. She swallowed.

"Yes." With her whispered word, a slow smile tilted the corners of Ethan's lips. His hand stroked across her stomach, and her legs parted. Her eyes fluttered shut.

"Look at me," Ethan murmured.

Her eyes fluttered open, surrendering to the intensity of his gaze.

Ethan's body claimed hers in a slow slide.

Cara gasped.

"Cara mia," Ethan whispered. The intimacy of their bodies moving together was matched by the connection of their souls as his mouth met hers in a drugging kiss.

Cara was falling, losing herself in the perfection of the moment, the knowledge that she couldn't deny the truth to herself any longer.

She mustn't read more into his words than he'd meant. He'd always said he loved her. They were friends, had always been friends. He couldn't mean he loved her the way she wanted him to, the way she loved him.

But on cresting the wave together, staring into each other's eyes, his soul was as naked as their bodies, and for a foolish moment, Cara let herself believe what her heart wanted, and showed him she loved him too.

FIFTEEN

Cara woke to a hand on her shoulder.

Ethan stood by the bed, fully dressed. "It's the last day of filming. If all the rushes are okay, this movie is wrapping tonight." He sat down next to her and kissed her neck. "When I get home, I'm taking you out for dinner."

He'd be exhausted. "I could cook?"

Ethan shook his head. "No, I'll be hungry. Better not risk it," he teased.

Cara scooted up in bed. "I'm not that bad a cook you know, I've been practicing while you've been away."

One dark eyebrow arched.

"Well, I'm not great either," she admitted. "Maybe we could get a takeaway?"

Ethan glanced at the clock. "I better run, the car is waiting. What are you going to do today? You can take the car if you like."

"I thought I'd read for a while." She reached for the paperback on the bedside table. "I've almost finished Juliet's book. I'm dying to see what happens."

Ethan ran a hand through his hair, and stood. "I got a text from Maggie last night. Apparently we've been invited to a party tomorrow night. At Stephen Brightman's."

Excitement bubbled through Cara's veins. Her first, and no doubt last, Hollywood party. Luckily, she'd brought the perfect dress, never really thinking she'd have the opportunity to wear it.

"I guess this means you'll need to go shopping?" Ethan asked.

"No, I don't think so."

Ethan kissed her quickly and squeezed her upper arm. "You're the only woman I've ever known who would pass up a chance at a shopping trip." He glanced at his watch. "See you later." And with that, he was gone.

Yet another example of how different she was from his usual girlfriends. She had no job, no prospect of one, and fairly scant savings, which would be taking a hit for the ticket home again.

Cara sighed, and pulled the duvet up to her chin. There was no way she was splurging on a dress she didn't need. No doubt Ethan's other girlfriends had been quite happy to let him pay for their clothes too. The mere idea irritated. There had to be some way she could use her English degree—maybe teaching a night class, or teaching foreign students English.

Her job prospects in Donabridge were non-existent. But maybe in Dublin... She rubbed her palms over her eyes. The school would have to give her a reference. She'd been a good teacher. She couldn't let one ridiculous incident change her life so completely. She needed to come up with a plan for her future. And quick.

She picked up Juliet's book. At least she could finish the book, so if Juliet was at Brightman's party she could talk about it knowledgeably.

IN THE MOMENTS BETWEEN TAKES, Ethan's mind returned relentlessly to the previous night. He'd asked Cara if she knew he loved her. And all she'd said was yes. She hadn't told him she loved him too.

She was so matter of fact this morning. So

detached, as though his words of the night before had meant nothing. Or as if she didn't want to acknowledge that her best friend had fallen in love, reneged on their agreement to have a couple of weeks of fun and not let it affect their relationship.

Ethan stood and paced his trailer. Eleven steps, end to end. Then eleven back.

He swiveled and kept walking.

There was no way they could go back to being just friends. Not now. She had no job to go back to. No one waiting for her back home who needed her as much as he did. He crossed his arms and whistled tunelessly as he paced.

When he got home, they were going to talk about it. He didn't want her to leave. She needed to know and truly understand how much he loved her. How vital to him she was. He'd tried yesterday, but somehow it hadn't got through. The thought that maybe she wasn't ready, or worse still, didn't want more than a quick fling wasn't something he was prepared to consider.

Whatever her reservations, he'd overcome them.

A rap on the trailer door.

At his shout, the door swung open. Maggie stood in the doorway. "Ethan, have you got a minute?"

Ethan nodded.

She sank onto the nearest chair. "You've been getting a lot of calls on your cell. From Aoife Fitzpatrick, I guess she still has your number." Her mouth stretched in a grimace. "I've spoken to her and told her you're unavailable, but she just keeps calling. Eight times at last count."

Ethan resisted the urge to punch the wall. "What does she want?"

Maggie shrugged. Her eyebrows pulled together like acrobatic caterpillars. "She keeps saying she needs to talk to you urgently." Her nose wrinkled, and her lip curled. "All delivered in a rather weepy voice."

The last thing he needed was to play therapist to Aoife. She hadn't even had the guts to tell him face to face that she was moving out and moving in with Zane, had just done the deed while he was at work, and left him a Dear Ethan letter.

But if he didn't call, she'd keep ringing his cell. It wasn't fair that Maggie should have to keep dealing with it.

"Pass it over then." He extended his hand, palm up.

"I'll be outside." She gave a pointed look, which he interpreted as 'and I'll make sure no one barges in.'

Ethan sat down, propped his Converse clad feet on the table, and crossed his ankles. He punched a couple of buttons, and reminded himself she must be hurting. And a gentleman never kicked a person when they were down. Especially if they were a girl.

"Aoife? It's Ethan."

"Ethan?" her high breathy voice dissolved in a flurry of feminine sobs. Not great, big, ugly gulping sobs, but pretty sounding ones.

"You've been calling me," he said.

"I made the most awful mistake, Ethan. Zane—"

"I heard."

"He cheated on me." A tough note crept into her voice. "He's played me for a fool. I need my friends, Ethan. I need to move out, and I need somewhere to stay...some support. I thought maybe..."

Ethan couldn't believe what he was hearing. Did she really for one moment think—

"You and I had something special, Ethan. I shouldn't have walked away."

"Hold up." He couldn't for one moment let her continue. He forced calm into his voice, and clenched his hand into a fist. "You and I are history. *Ancient* history. I'm sorry things haven't worked out for you, but you can't stay with me."

"This crap the papers have been spouting about you and Cara can't be true, Ethan?" She laughed—a tight, brittle sound. "I know you two are friends, but *Cara...*"

"I'm sorry not to be able to help, Aoife." Ethan's voice sounded coldly dismissive, even to his own ears. "But I'm sure you'll find someone."

He hung up, pushed open the trailer door, and handed his cell to Maggie. "She won't be back."

AFTER A MORNING FINISHING Juliet's book, Cara decided to flex her literary muscles by writing a detailed summary of it for Ethan. He didn't read as fast as she did, and had so little free time that she knew he'd find it helpful. He was due to go for a screen-test the following week, and Manny had said he was expecting the script any day now.

Knowing as much as possible about Juliet's book prior to the party could only work in his favor.

As the printer churned out the pages of the summary, Cara gazed at the cirrus clouds streaking the sky, as her mind flashed back to the events of the previous night. Ethan had told her he loved her while they were making love. It would be so easy to just accept him at his words, but something held her back, made her scared to believe it.

Shifting their friendship into romance was easy. But the prospect of really loving him, without any guard on her fragile heart, was terrifyingly difficult. Ethan lived in a different world, with a satisfying job, a beautiful house, and a life. Hers had been turned upside down, and although it would be easy to merely be—girlfriend, or companion—it wasn't enough. She needed to steady her feet on solid ground again. Needed to be in control of her life rather than just washing back and forward like flotsam floating on the tide.

She'd spoken to her family before she left. Had told them that she was going for a short holiday with Ethan. If she didn't return to Donabridge, all the rumors that she had once again fallen recklessly into the arms of a bad-boy would be confirmed. And no doubt her brothers would be out to America on the next plane, to question Ethan about his intentions.

She hissed out a breath.

There was nothing for it. She would have to stick to the original plan. Spend two weeks here, and then return to Donabridge and determine exactly what path the rest of her life would take.

Before she weakened she logged on to the internet, booked a ticket a week hence, and started the clock ticking to her departure. That done, the day stretched out before her, long hours of freedom and solitude. Being out and about with Ethan over the weekend had been such fun, but there was still so much to do and see that the prospect of another day on the beach held little appeal. The car had a sat-nav, why not just head out, make a day of it?

She'd picked up a guidebook in a little shop near Malibu pier, and now flicked through it. The Getty Villa was nearby, a wonderful collection of antiquities showcased in a replica Neapolitan Villa, with herb gardens laid out just as they would have been in Roman times.

Scooping her bag from the table, she picked up Ethan's car keys, and headed for the front door.

THE HOUSE WAS in darkness as Ethan's driver pulled up outside. Despite his best intentions, the last day of filming had overshot. He'd had to call Cara and cancel their dinner plans. She'd sounded bright on the phone.

"Do you want me to leave something for you?" she'd asked. "Because I made some dinner..."

He should have called earlier. But somehow he'd been hoping things would magically improve and he'd be back before nightfall. "I'll eat here." The talk would have to wait too. "Sorry, honey."

"Don't worry about it," she said. "I'm pretty exhausted, I went out today."

Ethan tensed. "You didn't have any problems?"

"I didn't even catch a glimpse of anyone with a camera. We must be old news. Your agent was right, it seems that the press have moved on."

Ethan propped his feet up on the table in his trailer, and wished she was with him. Talking on the phone was a poor substitute. "Where did you go?"

"Ancient Naples."

She sounded as though she was smiling.

"The Getty Villa?"

She laughed. "It's amazing, isn't it? Then after I found a little outdoor farmers market and bought some yummy stuff for the fridge."

"Don't wait up."

Apparently, she hadn't. Ethan climbed out of the Mercedes and handed an envelope to the driver. "Thanks for ferrying me around, Mike."

The driver's eyebrows rose. "It's all taken care of, Mr. Quinn, you don't have to..."

Ethan nodded. "I know." He grinned. "Thanks, Mike.

"Thank *you*." Mike stuffed the envelope into his jacket and smiled back. Then, with a salute, turned the car outside the house, and left.

The engine faded into silence as Ethan walked to the front door and let himself in. Even though Cara must be sleeping in the bedroom, the house felt empty. He flicked on a light and glanced around. Night after night, he'd come back to an empty house without for one moment missing the presence of another. Day after day, he got up, showered, and went to work. Filming was over. Tomorrow, there would be no car to take him away.

Tomorrow, it would just be him and Cara.

He locked the door, and went to find her.

SIXTEEN

"Might Harrison Ford be there?"

Cara'd pinned her hair back with a couple of jeweled clips she'd found somewhere. The different hairstyle emphasized her cheekbones. Her eyes sparkled, and her eyelashes looked longer somehow. A faint sheen of pink shone on her lips. Ethan peered closer. "Have you put makeup on for Ford?" he growled.

Cara's dimple made an appearance. "Or Mr. Jackman, I reckon if he's there..."

Ethan frowned, and advanced on her like a lion pouncing on a gazelle. "All these men better damn well understand—" he snaked his arms around her and tugged her close—"you're *my woman.*"

Cara squirmed. Her body shook with laughter.

"I see a remake of Tarzan in your future," she teased. "You've got him off to a tee."

"Me Tarzan," Ethan muttered in her ear, breathing in her musky perfume.

She sighed, and tilted her head back as he nibbled his way down her neck. "Oh wow. Me Jane." Her back arched, pushing her breasts against his chest.

Ethan's body reacted—raw, primitive desire making him wish he had time to rip off her shimmering party dress and drag her back to bed.

He pressed his mouth against the spot where her neck became her shoulder. Loosened his grip, and regretfully, pulled away. "We'll have to delay this until later."

Her eyes were dark with desire. She pouted. "Huh. Later you'll be thinking about the new movie."

He kissed her carefully, so as not to muss her lipstick. "I'll be thinking of you." His gaze traveled the length of her, perfectly showcased in the black dress that clung to every curve. "I'm always thinking of you."

Pink swept Cara's cheeks. She glanced away.

What was it? Was he coming on too strong?

"Cara?"

Her gaze returned to his. "I have to go back." Her lips pressed together. "My family will be worried if I stay here for longer than I'd said."

"We can talk about it later." Getting into a discussion about their future when they should be in the car heading to a party was a very bad idea. Especially if she was going to insist she went home soon. He needed to persuade her, tell her he wasn't going to let her go so easily. And he needed all his powers of persuasion to do it. Which involved getting her naked.

"I've booked a ticket." The words hung in the air between them. "I know you want me to stay longer..."

Stay longer? He'd been thinking about her staying forever. But obviously she hadn't.

Ethan's hands dropped to his sides.

"Look—" Distress flared in her azure eyes. She could read his body language as easily as he could read hers, apparently. The legacy of years of friendship. "Ethan, my life is upside down, I need to sort things out, need to find myself. We both knew this was just a temporary thing between us..."

Cold steel squeezed around Ethan's heart. He took a step back. "Fine." He turned away, not willing to give her even the chance of reading his feelings if she didn't return them.

Her hand grasped his arm. "I was planning on coming back." Her voice was low and quiet.

"What do you think your family will take that?" For years, she'd lived her life living up to her parents' and brothers' expectations. She'd dated Michael because her father thought he was suitable. Trained as a teacher, because it was a respectable profession for a woman to have in Donabridge. And had been devastated when scandal had struck and irrevocably shattered her life.

Now, instead of embracing all that her life could be, she was running back to try to put the pieces of a proper life back together. Her family had never approved of Ethan, not really. They'd tolerated his friendship with Cara because she'd been adamantly determined not to give him up. But the prospect of adding a bad-boy to the family ranks wasn't one that they'd accept easily. And unfortunately Cara didn't seem to have the courage to take a chance.

Cara bit her lip. "I can't just let them read the papers and believe what they will, I have to see them, reassure them..."

"Are you ashamed?" he ground out through gritted teeth. "Or do you even intend to tell them that our friendship has altered to friends with benefits?"

Cara's eyes widened. "We're not just friends with benefits."

"Really?" Ethan arched a brow. "What else would you call us?"

Cara's fingers fiddled with the bracelet at her wrist. "You know I care for you. You're the most important person in my life, I just can't..." She broke off and stared with eyes glistening with unshed tears.

Just can't take a chance. On love. On him.

"We have a few days left?"

She nodded.

"Let's enjoy them." He grabbed her hand, and walked her out to the car.

"I COULDN'T BELIEVE my eyes when I saw Ethan pick you up from the airport," Juliet said.

They were sitting on a small gilt sofa in a quiet corner of Stephen's airy sitting room. Long glass doors were open to the garden, and beautiful people Cara recognized from film and TV filled every available inch.

Juliet leaned closer. "When Stephen suggested him for *Edge of Night*, I wasn't sure," she murmured quietly. "But watching him now, I can see how he'd be just perfect for the role."

Cara glanced over to where Ethan was deep in

conversation with their host. He glanced over, then returned his gaze to Stephen's.

"The character, Philip, is very reserved. Very deadly." Juliet's mouth curved in a smile. "Ethan seems to play very confident and take-charge characters. I had a problem envisioning him in the role." Her eyes twinkled. "He keeps watching you when you're not looking. And my goodness, he's a master of conveying emotion without words."

Cara felt a flush heat her cheeks. "I read *Edge of Night*, it's a great book."

Juliet smiled. "I'm so glad you liked it, dear." She patted Cara's hand.

"I actually couldn't put it down," Cara confessed.

"Between us," Juliet whispered, "Stephen is really keen to have Ethan for the lead. And now I've met him, I can see why."

Warmth spread through Cara's chest. Ethan had been in danger of being typecast as an action hero, playing against type would be great for his career. And *Edge of Night* was such a powerful story. With Stephen Brightman involved, the movie would definitely be a blockbuster.

"Where do you think it will be filmed?" The story was set in Ireland, but Cara knew enough about film making to realize that many factors were involved in bringing a work to the screen.

"Stephen says we'll have a look at Ireland and some other European locations too," Juliet said. "There are a lot of considerations."

Cara accepted two glasses of champagne from a passing waiter, and handed one to her companion. She clinked her glass against Juliet's. "Here's to a wonderful movie."

Juliet looked across the room, and smiled. "Ah, here they come."

Stephen Brightman was a fascinating man. Lean and wiry, with a graying beard, and glasses, his enthusiasm for books and film was infectious, and after a few star-struck moments, Cara relaxed and abandoned her natural shyness as they talked about books.

She and Ethan had switched positions, and every so often she heard Juliet's laugh as Ethan charmed her.

"You're very knowledgeable," Stephen said. "It's very refreshing to just talk writing. So often, I'm being 'pitched'." His mouth curled. "Everyone has an agenda, a project that they're trying to get me to have a look at." He eyed her carefully, then grinned. "Don't tell me you've written a screenplay —just don't."

Cara grinned back. "I haven't." She tilted her head to the side. "Although I'm beginning to think that maybe I've missed an opportunity. I could have bored you silly with talk of it tonight."

Stephen laughed. "So, Ethan tells me you're a teacher."

Cara's stomach dived. "I was. But after all the stuff in the papers back home..." She squared her shoulders. "I'm guess I'm what you'd call *resting*, right now."

Stephen nodded. "The press can be a bitch. I've had my share of it." He squeezed her arm. His gaze met hers over the top of the glasses perched on his nose. "So, what should I be considering for future projects—have you read anything good recently?"

He seemed genuinely interested.

"Well, apart from Juliet's book, I have read a couple of really powerful books that would make great films," Cara said slowly. She mentioned a couple of titles.

Stephen reached into his pocket and pulled out a small white card. "Could you do me up a couple of summaries? Tell me why you think they'd be good for me to look at?"

Cara slipped his card into her purse. "I thought you didn't want to be pitched."

"Honey." Stephen leaned close and whispered. "If you like them as a reader, that's a completely different thing than pitching me a project you're involved with. I'm always looking for impartial opinions. They mean a lot more than pitches."

A tall woman walked over and spoke to him quietly.

Stephen waved to a couple across the room. "I have to go and greet a couple of my guests. I look forward to your email."

STEPHEN INTERESTED HER. Ethan could tell by the way she smiled at the older man, and when he'd leaned close and whispered something in her ear, and placed a card in her hand, jealousy clutched at Ethan's throat. It had been a struggle to concentrate on Juliet's words. To act as though all was well.

Now, as he swirled Cara around the room, he tried to let it go, block out the familiar feeling of distrust. Cara wasn't Aoife. Not by a long shot.

"Stephen gave me his card," she said, staring up into his face.

"I noticed." Ethan's hand slid across her back, feeling her body's heat beneath the beaded surface.

She smiled, as if unaware of the tumult roiling inside him. "He's very clever, isn't he? We were talking about books." Her eyes went dreamy as she spoke about her favorite subject. "I've read a couple of great ones recently that I told him I thought would make great movie projects. He asked me to send me summaries of them."

Relief kicked. But still wariness lingered. "Surely he has people to do that."

Cara grinned. "You'd think so, wouldn't you? But he said he'd appreciate a reader's viewpoint. He says it's difficult to get an unbiased opinion."

Her lips brushed against his neck in a featherlike caress. Ethan pulled her close. "I think it's time to leave."

SEVENTEEN

Their final days together flew. Long days spent on the beach and in the sea, followed by long nights of passionate lovemaking. There was no more talk of the future. Cara seemed happy with the present. She'd been through so much, and their relationship was so new Ethan forced himself to hold back, to give her space and time.

On their last night together, they dined again at the little restaurant facing the sea.

The waiter brought coffee, and left them alone. "I'm going to miss you," Cara whispered. "And all of this."

Ethan bit back his instinctive response. His fingers tightened around the small white cup. "There's always the telephone. We can still talk."

He sipped the hot liquid, feeling the burn against his tongue, and glad of the distraction. "We're friends, right?"

It wasn't fair to her to ask for anything more. She obviously didn't want it, didn't need him as much as he burned for her. It was his fault he'd fallen in love, not hers. And he'd promised that nothing would damage their friendship. Talking to her, being her friend, would hurt like hell, but he owed it to her to at least try.

"Right." Her hair brushed against her cheek as she looked down at the table. Candlelight played across her features, lighting a gleam on her lips. Her dark eyelashes dusted across her cheekbones.

Ethan breathed in, analyzing the air for a trace of her scent. Nothing. Tomorrow, even the scent of her would be gone.

Her eyelashes flickered upward, and his heart thundered at the pain evident in her blue eyes.

"My family means a lot to me, Ethan. I have to see them, have to explain..."

Ethan jerked his head in a terse nod. "My parents meant a lot to me too, Cara. I know you have to see them." If he'd been there he would have known his father had surrendered once again to the bottle's lure. Would have been able to make sure his mother never climbed into a car turned into a lethal weapon by the driver's drunkenness.

As always, Cara read his unspoken words. "It wasn't your fault." Her hand covered his on the table. "No one knew. No one but your mother realized he'd been drinking that night. Sean—"

"Don't." He turned his hand over and clutched her fingers.

"I want to come back."

Ethan's heart clenched. He brought her hand to his mouth and kissed her fingers. "It's better if you don't." He couldn't guarantee her life with him would be gossip-free, she hated the spotlight. Scandal had brought them together and expanded their relationship into something more. She didn't love him, not really. She was so attuned to him that she was offering to come back to soothe him, as a friend would.

And the last thing he would accept was her pity. He pulled his hand away, and stood. "Let's go home." For the last time. The pain within would only intensify if he didn't cauterize his wounded heart. Dragging things out would only delay the healing—cause him more pain.

It was over.

EIGHTEEN

Every day for the past three weeks, the sun had shone in Donabridge. Cara barely noticed. Without Ethan by her side, in her life, the days might have well have been filled with grey rain.

She'd spoken to her family. Explained the lies and half-truths that had plagued her since that day in the fair. But held back one piece of the truth for herself. That she loved Ethan. And wanted to give up everything she knew to go back to Malibu and be with him.

It's better if you don't. His softly said words echoed in her memory. She'd waited for days that had stretched into weeks for a call from him. A call to tell her he'd reconsidered, and was willing to try again. But the call never came. As each day passed without word from him, a dull ache settled in the region of her heart.

She wanted to call him, wanted more than anything to talk things through. He'd said he loved her once, but he couldn't if he wasn't willing to give them a try. The worst thing was that without him, she'd lost the one person she could open her heart to.

Loneliness dragged through her like a violin string over a stretched bow. She wandered to the wardrobe, and flicked through her clothes for something to wear. She'd finally given in to Suz's pestering and agreed to go out to the pub with her tonight.

"You can't stay in forever," Suz had pleaded. "Come on, you'll feel better. I promise."

With any luck Cara could deflect Suz's questions. Avoid talking about the pain that swirled inside. The first week she'd been back, she busied herself writing summaries and recommendations she'd sent to Stephen, but now the days stretched out before her in a mind-numbing wasteland with nothing to give her any hope for the future.

Cara took a purple silk shirt and pair of tailored black trousers from the wardrobe. Going out couldn't hurt. The distraction might even help.

ETHAN'S FEET pounded the sand in a regular rhythm. He breathed in the salt air, hearing the splash of waves as they hit against the rocks just offshore, before swirling in semi-circular slices of foam topped water on the sandy shore.

The days of filming were ancient history, but try as he might, he couldn't banish thoughts of the small blonde from his head, no matter how he ran to escape the memories.

Each night, his dreams returned unerringly to her. The way she smiled, the way she smelled, the way her lips felt under his.

The beach house came into view. Ethan picked up the pace and sprinted toward it. He didn't trust himself to call her. Not yet. If he heard her voice, he was afraid his control would abandon him, and he'd beg her to return. Tell her once again how he loved her, and couldn't bear the empty life that had become his since she left. Putting a friend in such a position wasn't fair. But holding back was taking every last inch of his resolve.

As he walked up the steps, the telephone rang from inside. He took the last steps two at a time, and reached it before it stopped ringing, heart pounding with the hope it was Cara.

"Ethan?"

Sean's voice. Ethan clamped his eyes shut and gritted his teeth. His brother's constant updates weren't helping either. Why on earth Sean thought Ethan needed to know that Cara was losing weight and looking pale was beyond him. "Hi." He forced himself to sound relaxed. "How's it going?"

"I'm ringing about Cara." *So, what else was new?* No doubt Sean thought a phone call or a visit would change things.

Despite himself, Ethan couldn't help the words that sprang to his lips. "Is she alright?"

Silence stretched for long moments.

"She was in the pub last night..."

Ethan gripped the phone tightly. His heart pounded in his chest like a jackhammer. The last time Sean had said those words, their lives had been irrevocably altered. Their parents were dead. Ethan struggled for words. "Is she..." He couldn't finish the sentence.

Sean's rapid intake of breath was loud enough for Ethan to hear. "She's not hurt. She's not dead. God, Ethan, I'm sorry man, I didn't think..."

Ethan's heart jumped at Sean's words. "What? Tell me."

"A journalist walked in and claimed Cara assaulted him. I have to bring her in for questioning. I thought you better know, because it's in the morning papers."

Assault? Cara? Ethan sank down on the nearest chair. "That's crazy, why on earth would Cara assault anyone? You know she doesn't fit the profile, Sean. There's no way..."

"I spoke to a witness, her friend Suz."

Ethan pushed his hair back. He still hadn't cut it, despite the movie's end. She'd liked it long, and somehow cutting it was another reminder that their affair was over.

"Anyway, Suz said she'd finally dragged Cara out of the house for a drink at the pub, and a journalist started pestering Cara about you, about your relationship."

Ethan's hand clenched into a fist.

"Apparently Cara took it well, and didn't lose her cool until he started in on how you were a heartbreaker, with a reputation for lovin' them and leavin' them. That got her back up, and she denied it." Sean blew out a breath. "Then he made the mistake of calling you a tough bastard. That's when she punched him."

"She..."

"She punched him. Broke his nose." Sean's voice was tinged with admiration. "She's one hell of a woman. Unfortunately a photographer snapped the whole thing, and I have to take action."

Ethan stood. "She hates publicity, her reputation..."

"She knew the photographer was there, Ethan," Sean said flatly. "Cara doesn't give a damn about publicity any more. She's found something she cares for a whole lot more than what people think."

"I'm coming." Ethan hung up, and strode to the bedroom to pack.

CARA SAT in the interview room of Donabridge Station, and eyed the polystyrene cup Sean had just placed in front of her. She picked it up, and took a careful sip. Just as suspected, hot, black, and horrible.

She placed it back on the table a safe distance away. "Do you need to read me my rights?"

Sean shook his head. "I just need to get the facts, Cara. From your viewpoint. He hasn't brought charges." His voice deepened. "Yet. So. What happened?"

She felt more alive than she had in weeks. And liberated too. Her picture was in the local paper again, and this time, she couldn't claim the words accompanying the picture were lies. This time, however, she felt no dread, no worry. Just pride that she'd stopped the words of that worm of a journalist.

"I was having a drink, with Suz," she started.

Sean jotted down notes. "How much did you have to drink?"

"I'd had a couple," she admitted. "Soda and limes."

"No booze?" Sean's eyebrows rose.

"I was driving," Cara explained. "I don't drink and drive."

Sean scribbled something. "Right. So, you weren't under the influence of drink, then."

"No." She was under the influence of love. "This man stalked up to the table and plonked himself down. He didn't even ask if we minded him being there." She rubbed the side of her jaw line, irritation blooming again at the journalist's cheek. "He told me he'd found out I was back from America, and that he'd been doing some *asking around*." The words tasted foul, contaminated by the thoughts that accompanied them of a stranger questioning her friends and neighbors. "And he said he'd discovered that my relationship with Ethan was *on-the-rocks*."

"Hardly a reason for assault, Cara."

Cara gazed into eyes so like Ethan's her heart clenched. "I didn't hit him, then."

"Go on."

"He started calling Ethan names. He said he was a heartbreaker, a ladykiller."

Sean nodded.

"I told him our parting was a mutual decision. I thought that would be the end of it." She glanced down at the pock-marked Formica desktop. "And then he called Ethan a tough bastard." Cara's hands clenched into fists as the moment replayed in her mind. "He sneered it, as if inviting me to agree with him." Her gaze flicked to Sean again. "I lost it. Before I knew it, blood was pouring from his nose."

She clasped her hands in her lap. "I'm sorry, Sean. But I don't regret it for a moment. That slimeball deserved it. He *can't* say that about Ethan, I—"

"You won't let him?" Sean put down his pen.

"No. I won't."

Sean crossed his arms. "Do you love my brother?"

Cara felt her eyes widen. Surely that wasn't on the list of regular garda questions? She swallowed, and faced the question head on. "Yes."

Sean grinned. "Thought so. Now, let's work out how to get you out of this. The last thing I want to do is arrest Ethan's woman."

Half an hour later, Cara walked free from the garda station. Apologizing to the journalist was one of the hardest things she'd ever had to do, but there had been no alternative. She was genuinely sorry she'd resorted to violence—but he *had* deserved it. Luckily, the man had enough brains to know he'd crossed the line, and her apology had been swiftly followed by one of his own.

Her parting conversation with Sean replayed in her head as she climbed into her car to drive home.

"Ethan doesn't need to know about this, right?" she'd said, eyeing Sean.

He shook his head. "Too late. I spoke to him last night."

She started the engine. After she'd had a bath, and a grilling from all members of her family, she'd have to call him.

ETHAN RANG the front door bell again. Still no answer. He clenched his hand into a fist and hammered on it instead, feeling the wood shudder.

"Okay!" a shout, followed by the sound of someone rushing down the stairs full pelt. "Ryan, I was in the bath..."

The door jerked open.

Cara stood wrapped in a towel and covered in soapsuds. Her hair was tied in a messy updo, dripping at the ends. Her mouth gaped at the sight of him.

"Step back." Ethan stepped forward as she obeyed. He tipped her chin up. "What's this I hear about you getting arrested?" He frowned, playing the part as easily as he played Crash Carrigan.

"How did you—"

"An airplane, sweetheart." Ethan held back the grin that wanted to escape at the sight of her. He breathed in her familiar scent, itched to pull her into his arms, but not yet...not yet... "You didn't answer me."

Her tongue swiped across her lips. "I had an...*altercation*, in the bar."

Ethan tsked. "That's not like you. I thought you had a reputation to uphold in this town."

Her face scrunched up. She looked awkward, embarrassed. "Someone said something I didn't like."

"Violence is never the answer." Keeping a straight face was too hard, Ethan felt his mouth twitch.

Cara's gaze was on his mouth. "You know..." she breathed.

"That you hit him for saying something bad about me? Yes." Ethan reached out and pulled her into his arms. Her wet skin slipped beneath his hands, suds from her arms dampened his jacket, and he didn't care. "You deserve a kiss for that."

It had been too long. Too damned long since he'd kissed her. And if the way she sighed and wrapped her arms around him were any indication, too damned long for her too.

When he finally pulled away, they were both

breathing fast, and the blue of her eyes was swallowed up by the black lagoons of her irises.

"I'm here..."

She breathed in and held it.

"To post your bail."

Her body shook. She laughed so hard she almost fell over. "I thought you were going to say something else," she said, when she finally could. "God, I've missed you." Her hands cupped his face. "I've really missed you," she added in a husky voice.

"I'm also here to fetch you." Ethan considered teasing her again, maybe something about not being able to leave such a loose cannon alone, but gave up on it as the warmth of her hands and the slow caress of her fingers drove all coherent thought from his head.

"I love you," he murmured. "I can't stand being without you any more. When Sean called, I had to come, had to tell you how I feel."

"I love you too." The truth shone from her shimmering eyes. "These past weeks have been torture without you."

"You had things to do... If you need to—"

Cara shook her head. "All I need is you. Nothing else matters. I thought I needed to have a life, rather than just live in yours. Thought I needed a job, something that I'd created, rather than just be another hanger-on girlfriend. But being without you hurt so much, I realize none of that is important."

"I don't want you to be another hanger-on girlfriend either. Which is why I tracked down that reporter and gave him an exclusive." He kissed her soft upper lip, loving her familiar taste. "No doubt it's trending on twitter as we speak—will she, won't she?"

Cara frowned. "What?"

"Ethan Quinn can't live without Cara Byrne – will she accept his proposal of marriage?"

Her smile was like the sun breaking through the clouds. Her entire body seemed to glow as her arms tightened around his neck. "She will. She does."

And as she went up on tiptoe to kiss his lips, the world had its answer.

AFTERWORD

I hope you enjoyed this book. I have many other books available in large print for you to enjoy, do check them all out!

Word-of-mouth is crucial for any author to succeed. If you enjoyed the book, please consider leaving a review at Amazon, even if it's only a line or two; it would make all the difference and would be very much appreciated!

Printed in Great Britain
by Amazon